MW00714608

The Boys' Club

The Boys' Club

Diane T. Dignan

First Page Publications

© 2004 Diane Dignan
All Rights Reserved

First Page Publications
12103 Merriman • Livonia • MI • 48150
1-800-343-3034 • Fax 734-525-4420
www.firstpagepublications.com

Library of Congress Cataloging-in-Publication Data

Dignan, Diane T., 1962-
  The boys' club / Diane T. Dignan.
      p. cm.
  Summary: "Novel about a woman redefining her values and reasserting her
self esteem after unexpected collapses in her career and personal life"--
Provided by publisher.
  ISBN 1-928623-00-X
  1. Women--Fiction. 2. Loss (Psychology)--Fiction. 3. Life change events--
Fiction. I. Title.
PS3604.I398B695 2004
813'.6--dc22

                                        2004024795

To Carol:
a dear friend and an exceptional woman.

Acknowledgements

Publishing a first novel is a frightening experience. Suddenly, once hidden scribblings will be read by others; characters with whom an attachment has been born in secret will have their lives sprawled on the page for all to see. Though a work of fiction, the story becomes very real to the one creating it.

For this reason, it takes much encouragement and prodding to push a trepid writer to share the stories weighing on her heart. This story would not have seen the light of day without the assistance of many people.

I thank my precious husband, Jim, who is always my source of support and edification, doesn't laugh at my ideas, and listened to me read the initial drafts while we drove hundreds of miles out of our way en route to Buffalo. At least I knew then that the storyline was engaging.

Thanks to Mom and Dad for nurturing my love of books from a very young age, and for acknowledging my desire to write since childhood. I could go on and on. Of course, introducing me to First Page Publications didn't hurt, either.

Appreciation is due to my sister, Kim, for her willingness to share her artistic gifts for the cover of this book in the midst of her very busy life. You are a superwoman. Spread those wings and fly!

Thanks to my sister, Glenda, for so freely sharing her family with us and for her belief in my ability to succeed. I treasure her excitement and encouragement about the publishing of this book.

Gratitude is due to my dear friend, Carol, for her kind words, well wishes and enthusiasm regarding this project. Carol, as well as Lisa and Nancy, encourage me more than they even realize, by the way they minister to their families, engage in their careers, and rise above challenges to realize their dreams.

A special word of praise goes to Nicholas, Morgan, Timothy and Dylan who bring much joy and balance to my life.

A word of thanks goes to Carolyn Daitch. You gave me my confidence back.

Finally, I would like to thank the members of First Page Publications for their friendship and hard work to make this book the best it can be. I am grateful for Marian's interest and excitement to share this story through publication, and for setting a short deadline to force me to finish it! Sarah has been my mainstay throughout this process. Her expertise, suggestions and sweet disposition have been invaluable. I also want to thank Joe, Deidra, Mike, Victoria, Sarah and the rest of the staff for all they have done.

$\mathcal{P}$rologue

When the dance of life gains confidence in its step, when our movements become careless and easy, it seems it is then that God takes us by the hand to teach us anew. Though it is painful to leave the place of simple bliss, we are nudged on, with much stumbling and vulnerability, unaware of the new opportunities that lie ahead. Many retreat to the embrace of the past, to a comfortable state of predictability. A few trust the process until, with gradual expectation, they break through the uncertainty to a fresh and beautiful step, to a dance true to their own essence, freeing and expressive.

When that happens, we realize that all we had to lose was our fear.

The Boys' Club

Chapter One

Autumn sunlight splashed through crimson and golden-leafed maples gracing the road to Alex's bungalow. The avenue bristled with activity. Fair-weathered Saturdays would soon be in short supply. Neighbors lingered outdoors until hunger and twilight urged them inside for dinner. Dried leaves crackled and chased along the curbs. The scent of wet foliage and freshly cut grass mixed with the heavy aroma of smoldering charcoal, carried on the evening gusts. An eclectic array of stately brick English Tudors and charming bungalows, built from the mid-1920s through the post-World War II boom, created a setting of friendly warmth. Though the homes were older, the neighborhood exuded beauty created by generations of pride of ownership.

Life was ordered and abundant, especially now, so Alex was confused when, as she stepped out of the

1

car, a sudden sense of foreboding crept into her heart and sank like an anchor.

She stood in the driveway, frozen, waiting for the feeling to pass. A thick, cold chill settled around her shoulders and moved down her body, her skin tingling in response. Her eyes moistened with tears in response to the heavy sadness that smothered her like a blanket. She shook her head defiantly. Her mind raced to find a reason for the disquieting feeling that shrouded her, but came up empty. As quickly as it had come, the feeling passed and a bewildered Alex was left standing next to her car. Her inner voice rose to the surface of her mind and offered a solution. *It was only old grief breezing past.*

"I certainly hope that's it," she said aloud.

Today had been a well-earned day of abandon. Work projects and housecleaning could wait. She slid a plastic-enclosed hanger from the backseat and carried it past burnt-orange chrysanthemums adorning the front porch, through the airy home, past cream-painted walls and saffron pillows strewn about the sofa, past the blue Staffordshire vase overflowing with sunflowers on the dining table, to the bedroom. Like an adventurer at the end of a treasure hunt, Alex felt the satisfaction of a perfect find after hours spent in pursuit. The little black dress slid from its plastic cocoon and lay on the bed, professional but not matronly, seductive but not cheap. Tonight, she had to look just right.

Quickly, Alex shed her jeans and T-shirt and slid the dress over her shoulders. Reflected in the full-length mirror was the image of an attractive woman with a well-defined face and large green eyes. Thick, chestnut-brown hair caressed her shoulders. The eyes were compliments of her father; the hair had a bit of assistance from the salon.

"Not bad for thirty-six," she assessed. At five feet, seven inches tall, she stood just above most of her female cohorts and was naturally slender—this to the dismay of her younger sister, Amber, who had to work incessantly to maintain an average build. Perhaps not having to cook for a family held some advantage.

From its perch on her dresser, Alex scooped a brown felt cloche trimmed with sequins and ribbon rosettes and pulled it over her head. She loved hats. They represented an era of style that ended with her childhood, never to return. Though she couldn't muster the courage to wear any of them in public, searching boutique shops for a new find brought immense pleasure. Her collection included a black pill-box with diamond-mesh veiling, a lace-trimmed cream picture hat from the 1950s, and her favorite, a feather-adorned number with a crocheted snood from the Civil War era.

A soft padding sound rounded the doorway as Einstein, Alex's cat, entered the room. Like his namesake, Einstein's gray fur had been a bit disheveled when he and Alex first met. Thick fur pointed in every direction, Einstein had found his way to her back door, wailing for food. It had been love at first sight. Cleaned up, Einstein emerged as a stately gray longhair with a supple white belly. He sounded a greeting of "mmmbrrrap" and jumped on the bed for a closer look at the new outfit.

"Hey, big guy, what do you think?" Alex asked Einstein and rubbed his silky fur as he toppled over on his side, begging for a full rubdown. Alex immediately obliged.

"The boss is going to promote me to John's team," she sprightly announced, "and that means more catnip for you." At the mention of catnip, Einstein's head shot erect and he stared into Alex's face with expressive, gold eyes. Alex took the hint and started toward the catnip stash in the kitchen.

Suddenly, the phone shrilled. Startled, Alex grabbed the receiver, "Hello?"

The responding voice was instantly recognizable. Susan Duprey was, first and foremost, Alex's good friend. Additionally, she was the marketing director at the office.

"You almost gave me a heart attack, Sue!" Alex exclaimed.

"What? Oh, sorry," Sue apologized. "Well, there has been a snag. Paul is on call at the hospital today and an emergency just came up with one of his patients. Can you pick me up for the party?"

Alex checked her watch. "Sure. Be ready at six. That should give us plenty of time."

"Thanks, hon," Sue breathed in relief. "I'll see you then."

Einstein butted his head into Alex's shin.

"Catnip," she reminded herself and set out to complete the task.

Anticipation of the evening dinner gathering at the country club gave Alex a surge of energy. The past several months at work caused a frenzied intensity that seeped into every aspect of her life. Her nose had been buried so deep in projects; she had barely been able to acknowledge others around her. Now it was time to slow down, lift her head, and enjoy the rewards of hard work.

The evening marked a celebration of the addition of several new accounts to the firm. Charles Seaton, the Chief Executive Officer, had talked it up for weeks. Alex had done her part, securing a $100,000 contract from a tough prospect. Although she had joined Barringer Consulting Group as a junior consultant ten years ago, she had only recently started feeling the vitality of inclusion with the "movers and shakers" of the industry. The work, consulting clients in the throes of mergers and acquisitions, was demanding and consumed much of Alex's life, leaving little time for personal relationships or hobbies. She had come to see the company as a pseudo-family, a group of siblings with similar dreams and goals. Spending long days at the office or with clients intensified this feeling.

Charles had implied that a position as a senior consultant looked feasible within the year. That meant working with John Tierney's team with the largest corporate clients, and a chance for a considerable increase in salary. The year was almost over, and her performance certainly showed her ability to handle the role. She felt certain Charles would announce her promotion at the party. Alex felt excited energy as she prepared for the evening: styling her hair, applying just the right subtle shade of shadow on her eyelids, selecting the perfect shade of lipstick. As he did daily, Einstein supervised the process from atop the vanity.

"Amazing," she pondered to Einstein, "how much thought a woman has to put into her appearance." Einstein purred in response, butting his soft head into her arm. "A man can simply clean up and put on a suit. No one reads anything into it."

A woman's image is reflected instantly in her dress, hairstyle, her choice of makeup and jewelry, with some people not looking much past that, she thought. Opting for a classic style, Alex fashioned her hair in a clean French twist and applied a soft mocha to her lips. A subtle, desirable look would do nicely. Although those attending the party would be those with whom she worked every day and their guests, Alex felt festive.

No one at the office piqued Alex's interest, except perhaps Corey Foster. Alex had admired Corey from a distance since he had joined the firm five years ago. Her disdain for women who pursue married men kept her from acting on her desires. She had resigned herself to the fact that he would never be fair game—until the extraordinary happened. Corey had arrived home early one spring day to find his wife in the shower with the kids' soccer coach. He had walked through the office in a red-eyed daze for a month after the incident. The crushing divorce that followed had left him quiet and pensive.

Everyone at Barringer felt terrible for Corey. After all, he had such a gentle spirit and love for his family. A few of the guys arranged casual after-work drinks with other prospects, but Corey would have no part of it. Alex offered consolation but kept a professional distance. Yet, one day he opened up to Alex over lunch.

His wife, Karen, had accused him of being "too predictable." She wanted more spontaneity and excitement from life. He was willing to change. Perhaps sailing or hang gliding would make him appear more adventurous. Or, he could assume a more unresponsive, mysterious demeanor to add interest to the relationship. Nothing seemed to work. Karen would not abandon her new relationship, despite Corey's persistence.

"You need to accept yourself as you are," Alex had told him. "Most women prefer stability in a relationship." But she could see in his tender eyes that Corey cared not for what most women prefer, but for what would make his wife love him again.

Alex pulled into Sue's drive ten minutes early. She sat for a moment, the scented autumn breeze caressing her face through the open car windows, and admired the stately Victorian structure before her.

Dressed in buttery-yellow with cream trim, Sue's home glowed in the evening sunset. On one side of the yard, willow branches danced and whispered in the breeze. Two white wicker rocking chairs lazily beckoned from the wraparound porch, from which hung pots overflowing with coral geraniums. Alex envisioned debonair young men clothed in dark suits and top hats promenading and laughing, with fan-toting ladies in pastel silk gowns, basking in a life of ordered safety. Ah, for a time when men and women knew what to expect from each other. What a unique period in history to have lived as a woman, holding a place of honor and respect as the weaker vessel to be cherished and cared for, yet with the budding antici-pation of new freedoms just on the horizon. The women who first gave life to this home would be amazed to see their younger sisters sharing the dreams and struggles of a man's world. Generations of sacri-fice and determination had brought the added respon-sibilities of breadwinner to the lady of the house.

"Was it worth it?" Alex wondered aloud. A flash of blue emerging from the house broke her reverie.

"Talking to yourself again?" Sue laughed as she burst from the open screen door and hurried down the porch steps. Alex often teased that Sue had the vivac-ity of a hive of angry bees stuffed into her tiny five-foot, two-inch frame. She marveled at Sue's ability to stay balanced on heels while moving at such a fast pace. Sue approached the car, both hands adjusting her left earring. Her blue eyes were made even more expressive than usual by her royal-blue dress.

"I just have to feed Charlie, then we can leave." She spun around and headed back to the house. In the doorway stood Sue's dog, his strong boxer physique offset by soft, brown eyes. Sue's cropped blonde hair and blue dress disappeared into the darkness of the house, Charlie bounding behind.

Alex smiled as she thought about her friend. In Alex's opinion, Sue led a charmed life. She was married to an attractive oncologist, living in a beautiful Victorian home nestled in an upscale neighborhood, and pursuing a promising career—all by the age of thirty-two.

Alex may have felt a twinge of jealousy, but Susan was such a close companion that Alex felt mostly admiration and happiness for her. Their friendship was built on mutual respect. There were no other women at the office to whom Alex could relate as well. Many of them kept a cool distance, applying that female competitive attitude so often imparted upon attractive and successful counterparts. The few who did seem willing to establish a relationship led lives enmeshed with spouses and children, or were ten to fifteen years her junior and enjoyed different pastimes and tastes. Alex was simply not able to share in their interests or priorities. Sue, though married, had no children and led a life of independence that Alex found refreshing.

Sue opened the car door, interrupting Alex's thoughts. She dropped on the seat and her whole body relaxed into it.

"I'm ready for a night out," she sighed. "I've been in the kitchen since eight this morning getting ready for Julie's baby shower tomorrow. I'll have to finish decorating in the morning."

Alex had met Sue's younger sister, Julie, last winter at a Christmas party. The two sisters had laughed and teased each other while preparing hors d'oeuvres and serving drinks. Alex had silently wished for the kind of closeness with her own sister that Sue and Julie shared. Now, since she did not feel like discussing baby showers, she changed the subject.

"So, what's it like having a dog named after your boss?"

"Oh," Sue laughed, "We had Charlie long before I was hired at Barringer—though it does help me keep things in perspective." Alex and Sue drove for a while in silence, enjoying the sunset's golden flicker among the trees. Brightly colored leaves tossed downward on the breeze like ruby and citron jewels strewn along the road. Alex loved living in the suburban outskirts. While only half an hour west of the office via freeway, her surroundings were quieter, softer, and more scenic than the concrete and glass of Detroit. Traveling even further west, one entered farm country dotted with horses and cattle, apple cider mills, and quaint antique shops spilling from old barns. The quiet ride was broken when Sue suddenly bolted erect in her seat.

"*Guess* what I heard!" she almost shouted into the dashboard. Alex was not startled. Susan Duprey was the prophetess and mouthpiece of the Barringer

Group. Events were somehow mysteriously revealed to her prior to their actual occurrence. Her contacts as marketing director didn't hurt. Alex appreciated having such a knowledgeable resource, most of the time. She gave a wry smile, anticipating a tidbit.

"What?"

"John Tierney is bringing in a new consultant, a woman. She'll probably be at the club tonight." The smile left Alex's face. Sue continued, "Apparently, her husband's firm is an important prospect of Barringer."

"So, a barter arrangement," Alex quipped. "We give the wife a job, and the husband does us a favor."

"It seems that way," Sue answered pensively.

"Whatever happened to good-old conflict of interest?" Alex asked.

"It's probably a token job with not much responsibility. I don't know who she or her husband are yet, but I'll try to find out and let you know," Sue said,

Alex pressed against the headrest and drew in a long, deep breath. Sue's statement had set off the old "fight-or-flight" mode and she wanted to calm it before reaching the club. Her hands tightened around the steering wheel. Why did she feel threatened by this new woman, a complete stranger, who obviously was hired to secure business? Charles Seaton would never allow a newcomer to fill her position on John's team, Alex thought. Resting on that bit of assurance, she let out a sigh.

"Don't worry," Sue consoled her, "I'm sure you

could run circles around her." Alex was amazed at how often Sue seemed to read her very thoughts, to know what lay at the core beneath her words and subtle gestures. Having such a friend was comforting.

The country club's quiet foyer exuded masculine ambiance. Paneled walls surrounded rich leather furnishings. A dark tapestry rug in shades of hunter green, navy blue, and burgundy stretched across the floor. A stuffed pheasant guarded the room from the fireplace mantle, its cold eye seemingly surveying visitors, determining them worthy. Photos of current board members hung on the wall—a gathering of elders, few with pleasant expressions.

Alex and Susan checked their coats and approached the main ballroom, heels clicking along polished marble flooring. Bursts of male laughter swelled over satiny melodies from a string ensemble, and then receded to low-noted conversation. As the two women reached the entrance, the scent of alcohol and tobacco entwined on smoky vapors. The elegant ballroom was studded with round tables covered in alternating white and burgundy linen and bathed in candlelight. Crystal and silver gleamed in soft radiance.

"Alex! Susan! Good to see you," Charles Seaton beamed. One large hand was wrapped around a cocktail glass, a cigar poking out from his thick fingers. With the other, he reached toward the two women. The men surrounding him momentarily ceased their conversation. Charles caught Sue in his wide expanse, wrapped his arm around her shoulders and squeezed her to his side until she fought for balance.

"Help yourself to the bar," he said, pointing to the rear of the hall, "We want everyone to have a good time tonight."

"I think I'll take you up on that," Sue said, righting herself and hurrying toward the bar.

That was more to escape her boss's enthusiasm, Alex determined, than to actually drink. Two glasses of Chardonnay was Sue's typical extreme.

Charles looked down at his empty glass and, for a moment, he looked much like a child pouting because he'd reached the end of his ice cream.

"Speaking of that, I could use a refill," and he was off.

Alex nodded a greeting to the gentlemen before her.

John Tierney's cool acknowledgement and lackluster expression was softened by his extended hand. "Alex, you're looking fine this evening."

'Fine,' Alex thought. *How do I translate 'fine?'* She smiled her thanks and took John's hand, quite a formal gesture for someone soon to be her boss, for a man who spent his days in the same office suite. John was like that—stiff, reserved, hard to read. Perhaps his position required such aloofness. Alex turned to the younger man standing beside John.

"And how is Parker this evening?" she teased. She enjoyed teasing Parker. New to the consulting industry, he compensated for his lack of experience by an inflated sense of self. Parker possessed a level of self-assurance befitting his dark good looks and history of always getting his way.

"Great, now," Parker responded with a roll of his eyes. Alex quickly scanned the room and noted the absence of his latest female interest.

"What happened? Did Rachel stand you up?" Alex queried.

"Not exactly. We had a discussion about our relationship again and she didn't like what I had to say."

"Did the word 'commitment' happen to be a part of that discussion?" She probed. Parker shifted his weight and boomed a nervous laugh. Alex smiled at having hit the target so quickly. John simply stood beside them, silently analyzing the conversation.

"Well, some women are funny like that," Alex scolded gently, "We like security." John drew a long, deliberate breath and slowly exhaled.

Sue appeared at Alex's side, handing her a glass. "I thought you'd like a glass of Chardonnay." Turning to retrieve it, Alex caught sight of her boss and mentor, Riley Conner, seated next to his wife, Kathryn, at a table across the room. Riley slouched a bit forward and looked with disinterest at the spectacle before him. The candlelight's flickering shadows reflected a weary face composed with as much enthusiasm as he could muster.

"Excuse me for a moment," Alex said, moving toward Riley's table. Riley stood and pulled out a chair for her.

"You don't mind sitting next to an old man, do you?" Riley asked. Kathryn broke in with a laugh.

"Fifty-seven is hardly *old*."

"Older than that good-looking single fellow over there," Riley said, tossing a glance toward Parker.

Alex sputtered a laugh. "In the first place, he's much too young for me. In the second, I have no interest in him whatsoever."

"Oh, I don't think he's too young," Kathryn said, squinting her dark eyes to take a long, hard look at Parker. "He can't be less than thirty. Besides, what difference does a few years make?"

Alex could see her point. Kathryn was at least seven years her husband's junior, and her sharp sense of style and petite figure gave the impression that she might be even younger. From what Alex knew, Riley and Kathryn shared a close friendship and had enjoyed being married to each other for over thirty years.

"He's twenty-eight," Alex countered. *Though he acts like a spoiled teenager*, she wanted to add but held her tongue. "You two are starting to sound like my par... like my mother."

Kathryn leaned into the table to make eye contact with Alex. A rhinestone butterfly perched on her dress shimmered brilliantly in the candlelight.

"You have to excuse us, we are everlasting matchmakers."

Riley nodded in consent. "Look at our daughters," he offered. "We found good husbands for both of them." Kathryn laughed quietly at his comment.

15

Alex sat back and enjoyed her first sip of cool wine. For the past ten years, Riley Conner had been her executive manager, teacher, and confidant. Riley had made a point to encourage and promote Alex since she had been a fledgling junior consultant, allowing her to work side-by-side on his larger accounts. Watching him control a meeting, observing his thought process and creativity, Alex had slowly developed her own level of confidence and grew to become Riley's counterpart rather than his pupil. Riley was shaped by the generation in which men took women under their wing, and he provided an atmosphere of protection and calm security which helped her to enter a competitive, male-dominated society. She admired him for that, and for the upright and honest way he handled his clients and cared for his wife.

Sue appeared at Alex's side, her voice high-pitched and edgy as if brimming with news ready to spill forth. "Come for a walk with me," Alex followed Sue to the doorway and away from the room's loud chatter.

"I've found out who she is."

"What do you mean?"

"The new consultant. She's standing at two o'-clock with John." Alex discreetly turned her head in the specified direction and noted a woman talking to, or rather talking at, John Tierney. Words seemed to shoot from her active mouth, punctuated with open hands, palms up, pumping in front of her as if saying, "Why?" over and over.

"Her name is Kate Rossman, and her husband is the senior attorney of Rossman, Kidwell and Sparks." Sue explained.

"The law firm Riley has been prospecting," Alex stated. Sue nodded and raised an eyebrow. Kate Rossman continued to assail John with words as he stood, head cocked slightly, looking as though he would much rather be somewhere else at the moment. Her head bobbed enthusiastically in conversation, though her dark hair was so short the movement did not affect it. Aside from her jerky movements, her stop-sign-red dress made her easily discernable among the dark suits.

Alex and Sue took their seats at Riley and Kathryn's table. Riley rested his chin on his fist and watched the antics of the woman in the red dress.

"So why aren't you involved in that conversation?" Alex asked Riley, nodding toward Kate and John. John's head had fallen forward and he seemed utterly engrossed in his own shoes.

"Humph," Riley snorted, giving a careless wave toward them. "After two years of chasing after that law firm, there is only so much I'll do to win a client." Good old Riley. His principles had been stepped on and he would have no part of it. Or, perhaps he was just plain tired of it all.

Following a sumptuous dinner of filet mignon encrusted with peppercorns, steamed vegetables and twice-baked potatoes, the string quartet quietly packed up their instruments. A disc jockey stood behind an equipment-laden table, turning knobs and checking wires. Charles Seaton took advantage of the moment, his voice booming through the room, "Excuse me, folks, I have an announcement."

Alex righted in her chair. Could he be announcing her transfer to Tierney's team? Seaton liked surprises. It would not be unlike him to announce good news to the whole group without telling Alex initially. Her anticipation was quickly doused as Seaton motioned for Kate to join him.

"I want to announce our newest member of the Barringer team, Kate Rossman." Kate rose from her seat and briskly moved across the floor to join Seaton amid applause. Alex noted the man whom she had been seated next to was not applauding. Rather, he brought his hand to his chin and grinned in subtle satisfaction.

"Is that John Rossman?" Alex asked Riley. He followed her glance to the distinguished guest and nodded in affirmation.

"Kate comes to us from the Clark Group and will be assisting John Tierney on his growing client base. We are fortunate to have her," Seaton continued.

Alex felt a flush of anger but quickly restrained it. Clark Group was a competing firm, though on a much smaller scale and dealing primarily with tax consulting. *Don't jump to conclusions*, she thought. A soft chuckle rose from the group as Kate grabbed the microphone from Seaton.

"I know you're all anxious to get on with the party," she drawled in a rich, Georgia accent, "So I'll just say how happy I am to be here and I am looking forward to meeting each and every one of you!" She handed the microphone back to Seaton and scooted back to her seat. Sue leaned toward Alex.

"She reminds me of a beauty pageant contestant," Sue whispered.

Seaton, a man accustomed to always having the last word, could only respond with, "Well, folks, there you have it."

Finally set, the disc jockey broke the silence with a jolt.

"Here's where it gets interesting," Alex said, poking Sue with her elbow.

"I know. There is nothing like watching people from work on the dance floor after a few drinks," Sue replied.

The selections were slow at first, rousing couples from their comfortable seats to sway in each other's grasp, perfectly alone among the crowd. Then came bouts of rock-and-roll occasionally interrupted with more mellow tunes. Alex knew the program well. She had attended more wedding receptions than she dared admit.

The next set of slow songs brought Riley to his feet.

"I believe they're playing our song," he said, extending his hand to Kathryn. She smiled up at him and placed her hand in his. Alex watched the couple with interest. She had never seen Riley dance. The couple melted into each other's embrace and slipped into a soft step as natural as breathing.

"That," she commented to Sue, "is what I want." But as soon as she had uttered the words, Alex wished she could retract them. It made her sound weak, desperate. Sue didn't ask for explanation. They had shared this conversation before. In the guarded privacy of her heart, Alex yearned for a happy marriage—a steady, comfortable existence with a man of character. Very few people in her life knew of this secret wish. Most interpreted her confident demeanor and independent lifestyle to mean that the last thing she needed was a man.

"Hmm. You still can, you know. There's plenty of time to find the right one."

The song completed, Riley and Kathryn returned to their seats. A brief moment of silence, then the vigorous refrain of the "Beer Barrel Polka" detonated in the air. Kathryn grabbed Riley's hand and pulled him back onto the floor, her face beaming. He gave the ladies at the table a playful shrug as he followed his wife. Soon they were hopping and twirling around the room with scores of other couples.

"He's pretty good!" Sue laughed.

The seated guests felt the energy of the moment and clapped or stamped their feet in rhythm. Hoots and whistles carried across the room. Then a shriek pierced the joyous sounds, carrying a note of distinguishable fear. The room was shocked into silence. The music abruptly stopped.

Alex jumped to her feet. A group of dancers solemnly surrounded something at the far corner of the room, something on the floor. She peered between legs to see what it was. Had someone tripped? The person on the floor moved. A brilliant jeweled pin caught the light and flashed through the group clustered around the scene.

"Call an ambulance," someone cried out. This sent several people scurrying for purses and jackets to retrieve cell phones. A deep whisper floated around the room. Alex approached the group apprehensively. Peering between heads, she saw the form of a man slowly writhing on the floor.

"Back up, folks," Charles Seaton's voice rang over the crowd, his hands raised in the air. "Give the man some air." The crowd slowly moved back as the lights were partially turned up to ease the darkness. Her eyes prodding for an opening, Alex waited. There! She could see now.

Her breath left her body, holding the moment in abrupt realization. Kathryn, her face twisted in fear, knelt at the side of the man on the floor. Alex's mind whirled in thick confusion as it tried to deny what her eyes beheld. Snippets of the scene broke through to comprehension—a fist clutched around a white shirt-sleeve, legs alternatively bending and relaxing as the form fought with pain. Then, the face broke through the numbing swirls of bewilderment muddling her mind. Pale as a specter, shimmering with moisture, mouth open, straining for breath.

Riley!

"Please, please," Kathryn begged, rocking slowly

on her knees. Her hands, not sure how to respond, patted his shoulder, stroked a wisp of white hair from his forehead, and rubbed along his arm. Her efforts seemed to comfort Riley, who stilled his motion. He looked at his wife's face, soft eyes pleading, surrounded by statues with morose stares unable to turn away. Broken voices poked through the dull whisperings.

"Heart attack."

"What a shame."

"Hang in there, buddy, they're on the way!"

Most people stood at a slight distance or took their seats, paralyzed with the reality of suffering. One couple held hands in bowed prayer.

Warmth enveloped Alex's body until a heavy drop of moisture trickled down the center of her back. A moan escaped from her lips. She lifted a hand to her throat and rested trembling fingers there as if to stifle an imminent cry. The room faded to another scene, and she was standing on her parent's front lawn two years earlier, watching white-clad paramedics lift her father's lifeless form onto a stretcher. The hot summer sun, a stomach-turning sense of loss, her mother's wails all rose to the forefront of her thoughts like a nightmare thought forgotten.

The air around her thickened and reeked of warm bodies swathed in sweat and too much cologne. Tinny voices swelled and diminished in her ears. People became fuzzy shapes—the shapes became darker, darker. Alex dropped her hand from her throat and crumpled slowly to the floor.

Chapter Two

"I was never so embarrassed," Alex whispered as she rubbed the tender spot on the back of her head. Seated in her mother's kitchen sipping iced tea, the events of two days earlier now seemed a distant memory. The scene welled into her mind, then receded to the present moment.

"Well, at least you only suffered a few bruises," her mother responded, setting a toasted tuna sandwich in front of each place setting.

"Did you put in the pickle?" Alex asked. Her mother drew an adjacent oak chair, careworn from twenty years of use, across the linoleum floor to the table and sat down.

"Of course, have I ever made you tuna salad without the pickle?" To Constance McGregor, food made everything better. It was the ultimate peace offering, the mender of all hurts, and the expression of all desires. Fortunately, she was a master at making it taste

23

wonderful. "What did the doctor say about Riley?"

Alex picked a small bite from her sandwich. "I spoke with Kathryn this morning. An emergency by-pass was done and he is being closely monitored. He will be out of work for a few months, but the prognosis looks good."

Constance looked into her daughter's face with expressionless steel-blue eyes. "He's very lucky."

"Kathryn blames herself for getting him out on the dance floor. But the doctor told her the artery blockage has been there for a long time and that Riley has had other very minor attacks in the past. It would be like him not to say anything, to just plod along as though nothing were wrong."

"She must be glad to still have him," Constance said. Alex saw a shadow of sadness brush over her mother's face and then harden in an expression of subtle anger. She was wishing Dad had made it.

The soft lines around her eyes and mouth had deepened since Dad had died. Stillness settled over her mother's body as if it were asleep, the muffled ticking of the grandfather clock in the next room the only sound. Alex felt the moment was right. Perhaps her mother would talk about it now. Cautiously, she threw out a line to see if it would bait a conversation, even an acknowledgement, about her dad's death.

"You know, seeing Riley like that brought it all back."

"Brought what back?" her mother snapped, her calm demeanor shattered by the subtle reminder of the incident she so desperately wanted to forget.

"Dad's heart attack."

Constance abruptly rose from her seat, chair legs screeching across the linoleum floor, and walked to the kitchen sink. She turned on the faucet and plucked a coffee cup from the drying rack, and then another, her hands busily washing dishes already cleaned. Her back stiffened, she focused her eyes on the task as if blocking out the visions rising to the surface.

Perched in the drying rack was Dad's coffee mug, "Carl" written across the front in red lettering. Alex knew that his clothes still hung in her mother's closet, each shirt and pair of trousers a banner of stubborn refusal against death, against separation. Alex knew better than to pursue the conversation. A lump rose in her throat as she tried to choke down a bit of tuna sandwich. After several minutes, Constance broke the silence with a voice of strained pleasantry.

"Amber and Mike have agreed to come home for Thanksgiving dinner. I thought you could make the dessert this year."

"Sure, Mom, I'll make the dessert." Alex fought the heaviness that sat on her heart and the moisture welling under her eyelids. She grieved the loss of a mother she could talk to about her deepest fears, her hurts. She felt inadequate to comfort her mother's pain, unable to truly empathize. How could she, who had never been married, understand what it is to lose a soul mate, an intimate partner of over forty years?

Alex felt like an awkward juvenile bumbling through a relationship with a woman who has experienced life's cruelest blow.

"Be sure to make plenty. You know how Amber's kids love sweets." Her mother had recovered, now that a safe subject had been found. Drying her hands on a fresh dish towel, she pulled a turquoise glass pitcher from the fridge and topped off their iced tea before taking her seat across from Alex. She didn't ask if Alex wanted more tea. It was provided to her daughter in the same manner as had been repeated over thousands of childhood lunches. Her expression softened, her eyes shone with eagerness as she imagined grandchildren's playful voices filling the rooms of her empty home.

"What, specifically, do Ryan and Sarah like?"

"Well, Ryan, being only two, will eat just about anything. But I know Sarah loved the Boston cream pie I made last summer. Let's see if I still have the recipe."

"That means I'll be making two desserts. We *have* to have pumpkin pie."

Constance crossed the kitchen, pulled several cookbooks from the counter and dropped them on the table with a thud. "If you insist."

"Will everyone stay here?"

Her mother stopped rifling through pages and looked at Alex as if she had just asked for an extremely large sum of money or announced she was trying an alternative lifestyle. "Of course! Where *else* would they stay?"

"I have an extra room, and the sofa pulls out to sleep two."

Her mother shook her head at this suggestion. "No. Amber, Don and the kids will want to spread out after traveling all the way from Colorado. And Mike said he may bring his girlfriend along."

"Another one?" Alex groaned. Her younger brother was proud of his bachelorhood, but enjoyed bringing a different female to every family event just to keep everyone guessing.

"This one's different. He's been seeing her for almost six months."

"Oh, well," Alex responded with a touch of sarcasm.

"How about you?" Her mother lifted her eyes from the pile of cookbooks and stared questioningly at Alex. "Any prospects?"

Alex sighed and fell back in her chair. Here it was, the formidable, never-dying issue. The source of her mother's disappointment, she was sure, was the fact that Alex had never gotten married. Never mind that she had once been only a few months from the altar while attending college when a flirtatious medical student had enticed her fiancé right out from under her nose.

"No, there are no prospects." Alex retorted. "My job has taken over my life for the past year. How am I supposed to meet anyone?"

Of course her mother wouldn't understand. Married at twenty, she had never worked outside of the home. Alex knew her mother listened with detached interest to her stories of Barringer and the challenges she experienced. There was simply no common ground for Constance to share, no personal experiences to draw from that would help her relate to her daughter's life. Since Carl had died, she became even more reclusive and shallow, seeming to take little interest in Alex's concerns. All her life, Alex had counted on her mother to pass along pearls of guiding wisdom to help her face difficulty. Those jewels had suddenly disappeared when Dad died. Even though Constance now had plenty of time to socialize with friends or follow her own interests, she instead chose to exist within the walls of the past, in solitary reverie of what used to be.

"Isn't there anyone at that consulting firm of yours who is available?" she asked.

Alex was caught off-guard. The interest she felt toward Corey Foster had never seen the light of day. She had always made sure to keep any thoughts about him tucked safely away. But as she thought of him now, a wry smile surfaced.

"Well, maybe." Alex lowered her voice as if to share a deep secret. "There is a man whose wife had an affair and left him. We seem to get along, but I don't really know him that well."

"How old is he?"

"I'm not sure, exactly, forty-two, perhaps."

"Any kids?"

"I think he has one—no, two boys."

"Is he good-looking?"

"What is this, twenty questions? Yes. He's attractive in an ordinary sort of way. He has a good build, sandy-colored hair, brown eyes." Her voice trailed off and Alex squinted as if she could picture Corey standing in the next room. "He has a sweet disposition."

"So, what are you waiting for?" Her mother hollered in exasperation, throwing her hands in the air for emphasis.

Alex hollered back, "For him to show some interest!"

Her mother shook her head. Alex felt like she was thirteen again, discussing the topic of boys at the kitchen table, becoming defensive at her apparent inadequacy, waiting for whatever pearls of wisdom and experience her mother might decide to drop as an offering in her cup. For a while they sat without speaking as Constance shuffled through her cookbooks, worn by years of flour dustings and smatterings of wonderful concoctions in process.

"Here it is," Constance said, the Boston cream pie recipe now found. Constance turned down the corner of the page and slid the book toward Alex. She gazed at her daughter now with softened eyes. Alex knew she wasn't thinking about the recipe book. She could almost read the memories dancing across her mother's eyes like ghosts in the mist as each one took its place in the forefront of her mind. Mother and daughter gazed at each other across the table for what seemed a long while. Alex got the impression that her mother wished she could transfer knowledge by osmosis. She knew her mother believed Alex would never experience the fullness of womanhood until she became someone's wife, someone's mother. It was the normal thing to do—to be married to a man, not to a company. Why wouldn't she just say it? Why could her mother not share how much she missed being married to her dad?

The older woman lifted her iced tea glass with a thin, white hand. A simple gold band rested loosely around her finger, a symbol of the days of normalcy.

"Alex," she quietly directed, "Take some initiative. Don't spend your life waiting for others to act. If he interests you, let him know."

Alex stared at the remains of her tuna sandwich. Her throat suddenly felt filled with cotton. It had been a long, long time, but she recognized a faint sound. It was the sound of a pearl being dropped into a waiting cup.

Chapter Three

What Alex was about to do went against every grain of sense she had. Why not just forget it and let things continue on their merry way? She was perfectly happy. Well, almost. Certainly she was happy enough.

"Oh, what the hell!" She said to herself, then picked up the phone and dialed the extension. But with the first "brrrrungh" in her ear, she quickly returned the receiver. No, this must be done in person. Asking a man to dinner over the phone when he was only a few offices away seemed just a tad aloof. She drew in a long breath and closed her eyes. *You must be relaxed and confident*, she thought. Corey must see this for what it was—a casual, passing invitation. Let him know his response would have no impact on her plans, or her self-esteem. As she stood to leave her office, the phone rang with a welcome diversion.

"Alex McGregor," she answered.

"Get ready to meet with Seaton; he's looking for

31

a volunteer." It was Parker, in his usual sarcastic tone.

"What do you mean?"

"Someone has to handle Riley's accounts over the next few months. Seaton has already hit up everyone else, now it's your turn."

Alex was surprised that Parker wouldn't grab the chance to work on Riley's business. It would be a learning experience, if nothing else. "Why don't you want exposure to Riley's clients?" she asked.

"Are you kidding? If I spend my time baby-sitting for Riley, who's going to make my quota before the end of the year?" He had a point, albeit a selfish one.

"Thanks for the warning."

A wave of hurt washed over Alex. It bothered her that Charles Seaton would ask the other consultants to handle Riley's accounts before coming to her as a last resort. Why? She had worked alongside Riley for years and was familiar with his methods, even knew some of the people he dealt with. Perhaps Charles felt the clients would relate better to another man. That must be it. He was a bit old school. Still, Alex hated digging for motives to justify her capabilities. She wondered if Charles had approached the new female consultant before he thought of going to her. Regardless, her sensibilities told her Riley would prefer that she handle his business over anyone else at the firm.

The agitation from Parker's call gave her just enough gumption to head for Corey's office, but not before plucking a file from her desk as a red herring in case the conversation went stale. She slowed her pace just at the doorway and looked in. Corey sat swiveled sideways behind his desk, intently reading a document that rested in his lap. Alex slid in quietly and stood behind his guest chair for a moment until he sensed her presence and looked up. A mild upturn of the mouth, a brief softness in the eyes—was he happy to see her? He tossed the papers onto his desk and swiveled to face her.

"How's Alex today?" Corey remarked in a cheerful voice. His demeanor gave her the confidence to sit across from him.

"About the same as usual, other than nursing my wounds," she rubbed the back of her head for emphasis.

"Yes, that was quite a shocker the other night about Riley, poor fellow. I'm glad to hear he will make out okay." Alex dropped her eyes for a moment, searching for a transition that would lead to a dinner invitation.

"What are you working on?" she asked.

Corey leaned over his desk and tossed one of the papers toward her. "The Spencer acquisition, or should I say post-acquisition. We're looking for ways to enhance revenue." He shook his head to imply that the task at hand was not an easy one and leaned back in his chair. Warmth crept into Alex's face as she found herself admiring his strong physique, evident even though hidden by a shirt and tie. His brown eyes caught hers in a silent moment.

"I was wondering," Alex started in her smoothest

voice. "There's a new Italian place in Plymouth that I wanted to try this weekend. Would you care to join me for dinner?" *There, it's out. Let's see what he does with it.*

"Luigi's Place!" Corey leaned over his desk toward her. "I've heard they have great lasagna. Sure. I don't have the boys this weekend, so just name the time." The next several minutes were spent exchanging numbers and making plans to meet at Luigi's restaurant at six o'clock Saturday evening.

Alex wandered back to her office and left Corey with his contracts. She felt good, tossing the conversation around in her mind like a softball during little league practice. Yes, he was definitely comfortable with her asking him to dinner. He didn't act as though she had overstepped any bounds. Perhaps he was the more complacent type who needed a little nudge to move forward. A sigh broke from her lips as she sat behind her own desk. Her phone flashed its red message button and she retrieved what was missed.

"Alex, it's Seaton. Come down to my office when you get a minute." She rose from her chair to comply. This should make her boss's day; she had every intention of taking care of Riley's clients until he returned. Too bad Seaton hadn't saved himself the trouble and asked her first.

Charles seemed agitated. A frown deepened the lines along his jowls and creased his forehead.

"Have a seat," he commanded without looking up from his desk. Alex was a bit surprised when he rose and softly shut his office door. "I am looking for

34

someone to handle Riley's accounts until he can return to work," he started. Alex raised an eyebrow in feigned surprise. "Most of what he has is settled for now, but there is a considerable prospect he was on the cusp of finalizing that could really impact our numbers this year." Charles' strong voice filled the room and Alex wondered if the closed door made any difference. "I have always valued your abilities and work ethic, Alex. I want you to handle the business."

"Well," Alex started, "I had already thought this might come up and expected Riley's accounts would need some hand-holding, but who is this prospect?"

"The Tri-Plex Group. Riley handled their acquisition eight years ago. Now he has a shot at handling another one." Alex remembered the account well. She had cut her teeth on Tri-Plex when they merged with a considerably larger firm. Riley had involved her in several meetings between the parties and she had come to know those involved with the acquisition process. Seaton continued.

"Dennis Mitchell, the CFO, will be in town next week. He has time for a dinner appointment and has agreed to meet with us. Are you available?"

"I'll be available. You know, I've met Dennis before. I helped Riley with research during the first project."

"Great!" Seaton thundered. "The more ties we have into the account the better. Riley is sure to recuperate faster knowing we have saved his opportunity." Alex agreed. Wrapping up the Tri-Plex business for Riley would be an ideal way for her to thank him for his support over the years. She envisioned Riley's return to the office and could hear his voice affirming her efforts: "Well done, Alex. If anyone here could retain that account, you could."

Then a thought came to her. How could she handle this prospect, Riley's other accounts, and take on the responsibilities she was sure to encounter from her promotion to John Tierney's group? Perhaps Charles and John had discussed this dilemma. It would make sense to ask.

"Will there be sufficient time to work on the Tri-Plex account under John Tierney's team?" It seemed a reasonable question. Charles took a breath and looked at her across the desk, the fingertips of each hand alternatively pressed together and relaxing in a rhythmic pumping motion as his hands rested on his chest.

"I have been meaning to speak with you on that very issue," he started. "Alex, you have done an excellent job for us this year, as you know."

"Thank you."

Charles leaned back in his chair and looked at the ceiling as if the words he needed hovered there waiting for him to pick them. Alex wondered why he seemed a bit apprehensive. He leaned toward her and dropped his voice to a normal level.

"Since you have reminded me of the transition to John's team mentioned earlier this year, I will take you into my confidence about some changes coming to Barringer. But you have to keep what I tell you in confidence; it can't go outside of these walls." Alex nodded in agreement, her brow creased in confusion.

"Yes, I understand."

"We have done quite well this year, and our profit margin is healthier than it has been. However, it is not where the owners want it to be. They have given us until the end of the first quarter to reach a twenty-five percent profit margin, or restructuring will take place."

"Twenty-five percent! We're only at ten percent now! What kind of restructuring?"

"Some of our business processes will be out-sourced to make us more efficient and unnecessary spending will be identified and eliminated."

"Meaning our support staff will be terminated as their functions end."

"Not all, but a good number of them, yes."

"But how does that affect my promotion?"

"Well, we have been put on a hiring freeze and cannot adjust anyone's compensation formula until at least next year."

At first this answer seemed reasonable. Then, after a moment's thought, Alex realized a hiring and compensation freeze still did not address her question or make complete sense.

"Kate Rossman is a new hire," she stated in retort.

Charles quickly responded as though he had re-hearsed. "Yes, she was promised a position before the potential restructuring was communicated and, be-cause she had already terminated employment else-where, was allowed to join us." With this, Alex stood and walked to Charles' window. It was a cloudy day and the tinted glass made the outdoors appear darker than it actually was. Barringer's offices occupied the highest suite in the building at the fifteenth floor, and Alex looked down on several buildings in the complex. A smattering of oaks adorned an island in the parking lot below, and Alex watched as autumn breezes tossed their chocolate milk-colored leaves to the pavement. She turned Seaton's statement over and over in her mind and then turned to make eye contact with her boss.

"I was promised a promotion before the news. How is that different?" Charles' eyes fell to his desk, his hands toying with his pen. He didn't have an answer. Not a good one, at least.

"With Riley gone and with the commitment we made to Kate, I need you to work with us in your current capacity." Charles' deep voice almost sounded apologetic. "Though we can't adjust your compensation formula, the Tri-Plex project could create a nice bonus for you. Also, I have decided to enhance your title to senior consultant." Alex slowly began to comprehend the arrangement. Somehow she had known, but could not bring herself to think negatively toward her employer. Kate Rossman was given the job she had wanted, and Charles was trying to placate her with a new title.

Alex slumped into the leather chair opposite Charles' desk, not quite sure how to respond. The soft leather seemed to envelop her small frame, making her feel like a frail little girl who has just been told she had to give up her kitten. Anger quietly seeped under her cool demeanor as she recalled Charles' promise to her months before, the years of working late into the evening and taking work home on weekends, all of the time invested in learning and advancing. Alex leaned over the desk and stared into Charles' startled face.

"I know exactly why Kate Rossman was hired on John's team," she began, pointing an accusatory finger at her boss. "She was brought in so Barringer could finally acquire her husband's company as a client!"

Charles shook his head. "That's not true."

Alex pushed out of the enormous chair and walked across the room in agitation, arms crossed tightly over her chest. "I can't prove it, but I know that's what it's all about. You've given her, a rookie, *my* job!"

Charles just shook his head and repeated "No, no."

Alex calmed herself with a deep breath. "I have worked hard for Barringer for many years, and I will continue to do so. But I'm not going to stand by and let a position that is rightfully mine, that I have earned, be given to someone else just so John can get a new account. You just tell John Tierney that we can *both* work on his team." With that, she left Charles' office and returned to her own. It was a half hour before she calmed down sufficiently to resume work.

Throughout the rest of the afternoon Alex doubted her reaction. Perhaps she should just take the title, work on Tri-Plex and apologize to Charles for telling him what to do. Doing so would keep the peace and make everyone happy—everyone except her. Her pride and self-respect kept her at her desk. No, let Charles chew on her words for a while. Working on John's team would have given her many sought-after rewards: increased salary, greater prestige, and a chance to work on more challenging accounts. Why should she give that up, particularly to someone hired in from off the street?

Anger gave in to frustration and then disappointment. Alex's eyes moistened. No. She wouldn't cry. She must not show any weakness.

Sue appeared silently in the doorway, unnoticed until Alex looked up from her paperwork.

"Is everything okay?"

"Sure. Why wouldn't it be?" Alex answered. Sue entered and took a chair. Just seeing her there made Alex want to cry again.

"You just seem a bit preoccupied." Sue said. Alex wondered if her conversation with Charles had been heard through his office door. "It's almost five thirty. Paul is working tonight. Would you like to come by the house for some dinner?" Alex responded without hesitation. She loved spending time with her friend. Somehow the intensity of problems diminished to a manageable size once shared with Sue, who had a gift for keeping things in perspective. Even though she couldn't mention a word about the restructuring, the visit would be a nice diversion.

"That sounds great, but I don't want to burden you with cooking."

"Who said I was going to cook?" Sue laughed. "We're picking up carry-out on the way."

Chapter Four

Saturday arrived gray and cold. Only a few weeks before Halloween, everyone talked about the weather and if it would break so the kids could enjoy the door-to-door canvassing without freezing. Late October in Michigan brought a mixed bag of weather—the sky could be fraught with chilled gusts or it could be a still blue sky with warming sunshine gilding the silhouette of almost leafless trees. After a Saturday morning ritual of grocery shopping and cleaning house, Alex curled on the couch surrounded by objects of self-comfort. These included a soft hand-crocheted afghan, a cup of hot mint tea, a paperback, and one sleeping cat. Though Alex anticipated her dinner date with Corey, just four hours away, the strain of the past week left her feeling exhausted and wanting to be alone. She watched as rain, and an occasional wet leaf, pelted the window.

The conversation in Seaton's office replayed often in her mind. The workweek had closed with the situation still unresolved. She wondered if Charles would act on her angered words and allow her to work on John's team, or simply ignore the conversation altogether.

She sighed and lay back against the arm of the couch. It was there again, that sense of loss, creeping into the remote parts of her soul like a fine gray mist, casting aspersions on the dreams her heart desired. Not that long ago her heart had drawn canvases of anticipated moments, and hung them on display in the recesses of her mind. Like masterful oil paintings they had captured the scene, light, and movement. There was the bright portrait of loved ones dressed in their finest, admiring the white-gowned Alex as she glided down the church aisle on her proud father's arm toward a dashing young man in a dark tuxedo. Another showed her parents, seated near a Christmas tree spangled with shining baubles, reading to a pajama-clad toddler cuddled on their laps. Slowly, one by one, each beloved work of art she had skillfully crafted had been removed from the wall with forced resignation. The most recent masterpiece portrayed a confident, sharp, middle-aged Alex basking in the success of her labors. Would it, too, be taken down?

"Stop!" she yelled to herself to turn off her thoughts. Einstein jumped awake and looked into her eyes with an agitated expression. "Sorry," Alex said, stroking his soft fur, "sorry."

The rhythmic tapping of raindrops against the window lulled Alex to sleep; it was an unsettled slumber, the type that creeps up and creates a fogginess of mind that intertwines the realms of sleep and wakefulness. It was in this state that Alex sat up on the couch and was pleased to see her father reposed in a nearby chair. His pleasant smile sent a rush of tender affection through her soul. She smiled back, unafraid. He always liked that oak rocker with the blue cushions, she recalled. They began a gentle conversation of silent words broken with unspoken knowing.

"How's my girl?" he asked.

Alex's heart leapt with the sound of her father's voice, though she wanted to address the plaguing issue left from his death.

"You know Mom won't talk about you. She won't cry and it's been over two years."

"Yes, I know. She's not ready to let go. You will help her."

"I don't know how. I miss you, too."

"It will come to you when the time is right." His voice was soft and calming and Alex knew his words were filled with truth. "I look out for her still, and for you." Without words, Alex shared with her father her concerns about Barringer, and her anxious anticipation of a relationship with Corey. He leaned against the chair in a relaxed pose, as he had done years before during visits to his eldest daughter's home. Alex knew he understood her thoughts—not only the fact of them, but the feelings that wrapped around each story like a delicate spider web, transparent yet strong. When the thoughts quieted, his welcoming voice responded.

"Be ready for change," he stated casually.

"What sort of change?"

"You will experience some loss, but it will make you stronger. Continue to work toward your goals, and keep your emotions under control. That is important."

Alex did not want loss. These words, though spoken with love and concern, were hard to accept. She looked away for a moment to catch a glint of sunlight on the window, reflecting prisms in the raindrops lingering there. The rain clouds had moved on. The sun's crystal-white light became blinding, and her father's presence became shadowed in contrast. Alex blinked against the growing light and was at once awake, the afternoon sunlight spilling through the living room window to rest on her face. She drew a breath and bolted upright. The rocking chair was empty.

Perplexing thoughts obscured her mind and she struggled to quiet them, to remember. Had he really been there or was she just dreaming? What was she going to lose? Would someone else die? The words became clear as the remembrance of her father's voice echoed within. Yes, he had been there. Alex lifted her hand to her face and cradled her head, eyes closed, trying to retain the feeling, the sound of his voice, the tender look of his face, as one strains to recall a dream. She couldn't remember crying, yet her cheeks were wet with tears.

The restaurant was bustling, and Alex was glad to have made reservations. Recovered from her nap, she glowed in a harvest-yellow sweater and brown slacks. Her mood had shifted, as had the day. The gray skies had cleared and now the setting sun rested in a pool of pink chiffon clouds in a pale blue sky. Once inside, the hostess led her through the softly lighted restaurant to a cozy booth where Corey sat waiting. He stood as she approached. Alex observed how handsome he looked.

"You're looking nice today," he remarked.

"Thanks," Alex laughed. "You don't get to see my casual wardrobe much."

"No," Corey took his seat. "Barringer really needs to lighten up on the dress code. No one requires suits every day. I've heard a few of our competitors have gone completely casual for the office staff and only require suits for client meetings." Corey wore a casual plaid Oxford shirt, but also a tie. A waiter arrived at the table with two chilled glasses and a bottle of Pinot Grigio.

"I hope you don't mind," Corey said lightheartedly. "If you don't care for my favorite wine, we can always order something else." Corey seemed in a playful mood, a side of him that Alex had not seen before. Could he be nervous?

Enjoying an appetizer of baked Brie and fruit, they talked mostly of work and of Riley's experience. A brief respite came at dinner. Alex twisted angel hair pasta around her fork and tried to think of a subject that would not carry the conversation back to Barringer or, worse yet, to Karen. Corey must have sensed her thoughts.

"So, what do you like to do for fun when you're not working?" Alex had to think a bit about that one. She had not done much other than work for the past year.

"I enjoy reading, getting together with Sue, shopping, jogging when I can find the time, the usual stuff." How boring and average that all sounded. Corey probed further.

"What do you shop for?"

"Well, since you ask, I do enjoy poking around in unusual shops and boutiques, particularly looking for hats."

Corey nodded, and then took another bite of his lasagna. "But I've never seen you wear a hat," he protested.

"Oh, I don't wear them. I collect them, though my collection is limited to about four. Something about finding a beautiful hat from another time is like a hidden treasure for me, it really lifts my spirits. Perhaps the trait comes from my grandmother. I remember her saying, 'Whenever you're really down, just go out and buy another hat.'"

Corey chuckled. Alex found him refreshing. He seemed genuinely interested in getting to know her personally, rather than going on about himself.

"And what sort of interests do you have?" she quipped.

"The boys keep me pretty busy. Jason is eight and Derek is twelve. This summer alone we've been camping or canoeing almost every weekend." He seemed almost apologetic, yet Alex admired Corey's love for and commitment to his sons. She wondered how Karen could have found him boring. He seemed full of energy and excitement for life. "We decided I would keep the boys during the summer and then on alternate weekends the rest of the year. It was better for their school schedule. I try to squeeze in a little golf, but as of late I prefer hiking."

"Really?"

"Yes, it helps clear the mind, plus, it's great exercise for those of us who sit behind a desk too much." He patted his firm belly. Alex noted that Corey didn't appear to need any exercise.

"I'd love to go with you sometime." Alex said, realizing that she had just invited herself further into Corey's personal life. She felt ridiculous assuming that he would want her along. Before she could backpedal, Corey had set down his fork.

"That's a great idea! You know, I'd love a hiking partner. While reflection is nice, some conversation would be nicer." He chewed a piece of breadstick and pondered this new revelation. "I'm planning a trip to the west side of the state in two weeks. Just a Friday-to-Sunday deal before the weather turns. Want to come?"

Alex thought about the proposition for a few seconds and decided to protest, though it did sound intriguing.

"Oh, I couldn't impose…"

"Why not?"

"Well," she stammered, "I don't have any hiking equipment." There, that was a good excuse. Corey was persistent.

"Can you purchase a good pair of boots?" he asked.

"Well, sure, I suppose."

"Come up with a good pair of hiking boots and warm clothes, and I can supply the rest." Corey seemed satisfied with his plan. Alex noticed a sly grin emerging and a gleam in his eyes. He was serious, and excited about the prospect of her joining him. Though certain his motives were above board, Alex wanted to keep things strictly platonic.

"What about a tent?" she teasingly asked.

"A tent! Yes, and a tent," he stammered. "You can use the boy's tent, but you'll need to pick up a sleeping bag. Tell you what, I'll draw up a list of what you should bring and give it to you at work on Monday." Alex was brimming with excitement at the prospect of spending a weekend with Corey, but playfully feigned doubt as she considered further.

Corey intently waited for her reply. "It'll be fun. I promise."

"No big black bears or other things that go bump in the night?" Alex teased.

"There aren't any bears where we're going. And if there are, I'll take care of them, no problem."

"Well, okay."

The rest of the evening's conversation took on a new energy as they shared with each other those private tastes and thoughts reserved only for good friends. They ordered a dessert of gooey apple dumpling, more to extend the conversation than to placate a desire for sweets. It was after nine thirty when Corey walked Alex to her car.

"This was a great idea," he remarked. "I'm looking forward to our hiking adventure!" With that, he extended his arms and gave Alex a warm hug. The embrace, though brief, was unexpected and sent an excited pulse of warmth through her body. She felt his rough cheek next to hers, smelled the scent of his hair at the nape of his neck. As Corey squeezed Alex close to his chest, a rush of emotion swelled in her throat and made her eyes sting with restrained tears. It had been ages since she had been on the receiving end of a bear hug. The feel of it was like liquid love pouring over her, surrounding her so that she had to hold her breath for fear of drowning.

Driving home, Alex pondered the events of the evening with a smile. The gloom of that afternoon had dissipated completely.

"You should be ashamed of yourself," she chided, "letting a little attention from a man have such an effect on you." She had to admit the evening had lifted her spirits and made her feel attractive and desirable. Tomorrow she would shop for hiking boots. Oh, and a sleeping bag.

Chapter Five

The week began slowly and methodically, with no mention of the discussion in Charles' office. A dinner meeting with Tri-Plex was scheduled for later in the week, and Alex busily prepared her proposal. Charles was to have joined her, but a conflicting appointment took precedence. Dennis was traveling from out-of-town and would meet with the Tri-Plex officers at their local office the next day. Part of this meeting would include his recommendation to use Barringer Group for their merger and acquisition process. It was not possible to move the date to accommodate Charles' schedule.

By Wednesday, it was evident that Charles had approached John Tierney about promoting Alex to his team. Perhaps Charles had suggested usurping Kate Rossman, but the result was surprising and fraught with trouble. Sue slipped into Alex's office and quietly shut the door behind her.

"Charles talked to John about you joining his team this morning," she began. Her manner seemed agitated, and Alex's interest was immediately piqued.

"What happened?"

"I don't know what was said, but John is packing up his office."

"What?"

Sue nodded, a look of incredulity on her face. "Oh, he's not leaving, yet," she clarified, "He is threatening to leave." Alex let Sue's words penetrate for a moment. So that was what it had come to. Either John got his way, which meant Kate remained on his team and Alex did not, or he would leave. Ultimately, that meant Alex would be left where she was. John held the largest client interest with the firm, meaning he usually prevailed. Charles did not have the fortitude to disappoint his greatest source of revenue, particularly now that the stakes were so high. John knew this, and was using it to his advantage.

"I'm amazed that John would be so dramatic in making the point that he doesn't want me on his team," Alex said.

"You are indirectly threatening his interests," Sue noted. The two women sat in stunned silence for a few moments.

"I wonder if this would have happened if Kate had not joined the firm," Alex mused. Sue simply shook her head, unable to respond. Once Sue had left, Alex slipped past John's office, under the guise of needing to fax a document. It was dark. Files protruded from two open boxes. His pictures had been taken down and stacked against the wall. Personal effects sat piled on his credenza: a coffee mug, brass desk clock, framed photo of his grown children, and a sleeve of golf balls among the litter. Rejection burned her cheeks and she clenched her fists. Let him feel threatened. She would secure Tri-Plex, and others, and leave John Tierney to sink slowly into obscurity.

Thursday afternoon was chilly but sunny as Alex entered the hotel restaurant for her four o'clock meeting. Dennis Mitchell would be waiting at his table. Her proposal tucked under her arm, she felt confident about securing this account. The hostess led her toward Dennis' table, and Alex recognized him immediately. As he stood to acknowledge her, she noted he looked older and thinner than she remembered. His dark, curled hair was now strewn with gray. She had forgotten his tall physique and gray eyes. She had never before seen anyone with gray eyes, pale like doves, difficult not to look at.

They shook hands and began with small talk. Dennis apparently remembered her as well, and she enjoyed his friendly demeanor. It added to her ease in presenting the proposal. They discussed business over rosemary chicken and chilled glasses of piesporter. The meal concluded, they sipped coffee and chatted about the upcoming acquisition.

"I have always admired the work done by Barringer," Dennis remarked at the end of dinner. Alex waited for the next line, for him to confirm his recommendation to the Tri-Plex officers the next day that they assign Barringer as their consultant. Instead, he leaned into the table and caught her eyes with his. "I admire you as a person as well, Alex." Dennis emphasized his point by resting his hand on hers. His gray eyes softened, as if a little boy rose to the surface and overtook the man.

His touch made her breath stop and her back stiffen. An invisible and delicate boundary had been suddenly penetrated. Thoughts twisted and turned in Alex's mind. A shield of defense rose in her spirit and stood firm against hot darts of female emotion. A nervous chuckle escaped from her closed lips as her eyes lowered to look at his hand, still resting on hers. Dark hairs curled on the spaces between his knuckles. A gold band encircled his ring finger, careworn and loose. He pulled his hand away and shifted slightly in his chair. Shedding the vulnerability of the moment, Dennis wrapped the cloak of male authority around himself once again.

"Though, at first I was just a bit concerned, not having Riley on the job. We have worked together a long time."

"Yes! Riley has worked with you on and off for about eight years." Alex was grateful to get back on the topic of business though a trace of worry clouded her thoughts. The waitress appeared with the bill and

Alex motioned to receive it.

"Oh no, I never let a lady pay for dinner."

"But, actually, Barringer is picking up the tab," Alex protested. Dennis was making another attempt to personalize the meeting, and Alex was quick to correct his assumptions.

"Well, then, that's a different story." He leaned back in his chair and watched intently as Alex signed the bill. She felt his cloud-gray eyes intently examining her every move. With the waitress's departure, he leaned forward and crossed his arms on the table, his face as close to Alex as the seating arrangement would allow.

"You're fond of Riley?"

"Oh, yes. I have a lot of respect for Riley."

"Then you wouldn't want to disappoint him. Rather, it would be a disappointment if Tri-Plex was no longer a client when he returned to the office."

Alex's eyes flashed with confusion and anger. What was he driving at? Why would he threaten her?

"Of course," she retorted.

"There is something you can do to assure Riley will still have a client when he returns." Dennis straightened in his seat. Alex listened anxiously, anticipating a fee negotiation to begin. Yet Dennis remained silent, drawing a response from her.

"What?" She shrugged the question.

"Come up to my room for a while."

Alex dropped her eyes to the white linen. So that was it. Her calm demeanor hid the shock that pulsed in her heart. A client had never propositioned her before. She silently searched for the best answer as her fingers toyed with the cloth napkin.

"I can't do that."

A moment of silence, and then, "Why not?"

"I'll lose my job." She lifted her eyes now and peered directly into his to let him know she meant business. She wanted to say something entirely different. *Why? Because you have offended me, because my body doesn't come with the deal.* Alex knew enough about men not to speak her thoughts. *Be careful. Let him think you are flattering him as you turn him down.*

"No one will know. I can assure you of that," he said.

"Someone could find out."

"Well, the chances of losing your job are greater if Tri-Plex moves its business to the competition right after you've taken over the account." Alex wondered if Seaton had told Dennis about the strain on Barringer Group and how important his business was at this time.

"That's sexual harassment."

Dennis gave a sly grin and raised an eyebrow as if to say, "You're kidding." Alex's mind raced for a way out of this distressing turn of events. She could just refuse and go back to the office tomorrow and report him. They would support her—wouldn't they? Words surfaced to the forefront of her muddled thoughts like a bobber on a fishing line: Riley's long-term account. Sell-out. Failure. Failure on Riley's account. She could just walk away and let them assign Kate Rossman. Let him hit on her. Alex pictured Kate's husband finding out. More words floated to the surface: embarrassment, Rossman Kidwell refusing to work with Barringer. The defeat would be blamed on her.

Okay, what if she did this thing and no one found out about it? Nothing. Life would go on for everyone. Riley would keep his account. She would look like a hero. But would it be the same for her? Restrained anger pounded in her ears. She clenched her jaw tight. She would not verbalize what she was about to do. Dennis swallowed the last of his coffee.

"Well?"

Alex gazed down at the table again and nodded. She didn't want to see his face when he got his way. Dennis rose to his feet and dropped a key card, still in its envelope with the room number written next to it, on the table in front of her. He must have had the foresight to ask for an extra room key at the desk. Alex smirked as she realized that his plans were premeditated.

"Come up when you're ready," was all he said. Alex looked up at him with a feigned smile and rested her fingers on the key. Dennis turned and left.

She ordered a cocktail and sat for twenty minutes—the fastest twenty minutes she could remember. During that time Alex wondered if she was normal. Wouldn't most women look forward to an evening of uncommitted sex with a handsome man?

Shouldn't she be flattered?

Yet all she felt was defeated and angry. Her years of hard work, her expertise, her willingness to help her employer, were suddenly reduced to being an object to fulfill the male sex drive. She shoved the room key in her purse and headed for the elevator. Scanning the faces around her, she felt her cheeks warm. Could they tell what she was about to do? Pushing the elevator button, a silly rhyme from her childhood echoed within...*Cinderella, dressed in yella, went upstairs to kiss a fella*. It's funny how those things come back at the strangest times, she noted wryly. The elevator dinged a welcome as the doors opened to the eighth floor. Slowly, as if in a trance, she stepped into the corridor and headed toward the room number. 810. 812... The next room was it, 814. She approached apprehensively and rested her hand on the knob while her other hand searched her purse for the keycard. *Made a mistake, kissed a snake. How many doctors did it take?* A vision from childhood flashed in her mind as the little rhyme echoed. She was jumping rope with friends from school. Her heart pounded out the rhythm... one, two, three, four...

Alex stopped fumbling for the key. She didn't need to do this! Her own convictions were more important than this account, than even her job. As of this moment, she was still in control. Consequences could be dealt with later. The doorknob slowly began to twist under her fingers. She stepped back in realization that Dennis was on the other side, opening the door. She had seconds to decide. Alex burst for the elevator, just slipping past the doors as they began to close. An elderly couple stood at the back of the elevator, gently holding hands. They smiled as she groped for the lobby button. As she realized the elevator was, indeed, going down, a deep sigh escaped from her lips.

"You just made it!" The elderly lady laughed.

"Yes, I certainly did," Alex responded.

The fresh evening air cooled her face and breezed through her chestnut hair as she made her escape. The earlier sunshine was now replaced with a velvet-blue sky jeweled by a glowing crescent moon. Gripping the steering wheel with shaking hands, she pondered what to do next. She needed to share what happened with someone, to expose the events of the evening and validate her response. So much hinged on securing this account. It could all be lost by Monday. As if her car were self-propelled, Alex found herself parked in front of Sue's house. Paul's black Saab sat in the driveway. She shouldn't intrude; the couple spent so little time together. Yet, the urge to share what happened was strong. She would stay no longer than 15 minutes. Sue's foyer wafted with the scent of slow-cooked roast beef and potatoes.

"You're just in time!" Sue exclaimed, "We're about to have dinner." The foyer, with its candle-strewn sideboard and warmly lighted kitchen beyond, drew her in from the chill autumn air. Paul rounded the corner and extended a hand of welcome. He was a gentle sort, the type of man that would be a source of calm strength to his patients dealing with the frightening intimidation of cancer. Sue and Paul's home wrapped around Alex like a warm blanket. She felt safe here; indeed, she felt loved.

"Oh, I've eaten. I won't stay but a few minutes," she apologized as Paul helped her slip off her jacket.

"That's right!" Sue responded. "Your dinner with Tri-Plex. How did it go? Did you win the account?"

Alex rolled her eyes in a look that said, 'Not exactly.'

"Stay and tell us what happened," Sue invited as she walked into the kitchen where the dinner preparations were under way. While Sue and Paul enjoyed pot roast and salad, Alex sipped hot herbal tea and explained the evening's events and its fateful conclusion. Sue's pleasant demeanor hardened in defense.

"You made the right decision," she declared. "What an awful position to be put in."

"Except that Barringer won't get the business, and how will I explain that to Seaton?"

Throughout dinner, Paul had quietly listened to Alex's story. Now he removed his glasses and rubbed his eyes in thought "Don't do anything just yet," he said. Replacing his glasses, he gazed at Alex with big, soft eyes. "My assumption is that Dennis won't carry through on his threat to take his business elsewhere. The board meeting is tomorrow and unless he has already accepted proposals from the competition, there isn't time for him to change his mind based on your standing him up tonight."

"But, what if he does carry through with his threat?" Sue questioned her husband.

"If the account is lost, then Alex can tell Seaton what happened. His first response should be to protect his employee. He should understand your position perfectly." While this was good advice, feelings of doubt arose in Alex's mind. After the events of the past few weeks, she no longer assumed that Seaton had her best interest in mind. Her concerns reflected on her face as she silently considered Paul's suggestion. Sue, knowing Seaton's mindset and Tierney's threat to leave the company, expressed Alex's suspicion.

"But that's the problem" Sue said. "Barringer is desperate for new business that will increase our profit margin. And with John Tierney's threats to leave, they could use this against Alex."

Paul proceeded, undisturbed, "I can't imagine Barringer making a business decision to terminate a long-term employee because she wouldn't accept a proposition from a client." Then to Alex, "Be sure to tell Seaton what happened right away, with a witness present, if Tri-Plex declines to work with you. Back it up with a written memo. If there are unfair repercussions, you should consider bringing a lawsuit."

"I'll stand by you, if it comes to that," Sue promised.

Heading home, Alex was grateful for Paul's counsel. She would lay low and see how things progressed, secretly wielding the weapon of legal action should things work against her. Surprisingly, Alex felt a peaceful confidence in her readiness to employ it.

Chapter six

Perhaps taking a cosmetic bag on a camping trip was overdoing things a bit. It certainly wasn't on the list of necessities Corey had given her. Alex reviewed the list one more time: sleeping bag (suitable for outdoors), thermal underwear (it can get cold near the lake), light gloves, hiking boots (or shoes). Not only had Corey provided a list, but a running commentary followed items he felt she might question. Three days would be spent in close contact with a man she very much wanted to get to know better. The make-up kit would stay just in case she needed a little color. Corey would arrive in an hour and her packing was almost complete. Admittedly, Alex felt excited anticipation about the weekend. She wondered how Corey envisioned their relationship. *Be cautious and level-headed, it's only a casual outing* she reminded herself.

As the week had drawn to a close, Alex had been able to set Barringer aside for a few days and focus on her personal life. Tri-Plex did select Barringer for the acquisition project, though Dennis had called Seaton on Tuesday with the news, rather than face the embarrassment of contacting Alex. The incident at the hotel seemed to be forgotten, and Alex was grateful when Seaton confirmed the acquisition project had been reassigned to the local Tri-Plex team. Dennis would be out of the picture for a while. Though John Tierney had not unpacked his boxes yet, a memo announcing Alex's new title of senior consultant had been circulated, along with congratulations on securing the Tri-Plex account. She had called Riley at home to share the news. He had sounded genuinely happy for her, and said he felt downright rested and pretty good for an old guy.

Today was Friday. Alex had taken a well-earned day off. She and Corey would drive the three-hour trip to the west side of the state that afternoon. Corey went to the office in the morning, planning to leave for an "appointment" by 11:00. "No sense in triggering gossip," he had said. Alex had just filled Einstein's bowl and left a note for Sue about his feeding instructions when Corey appeared at the door.

"Half an hour early," Alex murmured teasingly as she answered the door. Corey stood before her, dappled sunlight splashing on his light hair, a broad smile on his face.

"Hope you don't mind that I'm early," Corey

stated as he entered the house, "but you'll need to make a slight adjustment in your packing." This was his first visit to Alex's home, and he scanned the rooms before him with a slight grin of approval. Alex noted the wandering of his curious eyes. What did he expect? Teddy bears and lace, perhaps?

"Come in and sit while I finish packing," she said. "What do you mean by adjustments?" Corey sat on the couch, his fingers tapping the tops of his thighs with restrained energy.

"You'll need to pack something…" he struggled for the right term, "business casual—something other than hiking boots and jeans." Alex raised an eyebrow. "I thought we could spend Sunday checking out a few of the towns along the lake." Alex smiled at his thoughtfulness. He was creating an escape in case the camping idea wasn't a hit.

"Give me about fifteen minutes and I'll be ready to leave," she answered. "There's some iced tea and pop in the fridge if you're thirsty." Alex retreated to the bedroom and selected a pair of low-heeled loafers, khakis, a cream-colored turtleneck and a blazer the shade of pumpkin pie to pack for Sunday's excursion.

"Wow, that's some cat!" Corey exclaimed from the living room, followed by soft renditions of "Here, kitty." Alex grabbed her bag and rounded the corner to find Einstein seated next to Corey, both front paws resting on his leg, enjoying a head rub.

"I see you've met Einstein."

Corey laughed out loud. "I can see the resemblance."

"He likes you. Most people get snubbed the first few visits."

"Is that a good sign?" Corey looked up into Alex's face with an expression of vulnerable hopefulness. His eyes made her hesitate. Perhaps she envisioned more in his expression than was actually there. No, she read between the words to hear the real questions, fitting for such a time when what had been casual friendship emerges from the safety of its cocoon and a metamorphosis occurs.

When on the brink of potential deep knowing, of discovering the person with whom a lifetime of moments may be invested, the bruised soul asks, "Are you prepared to move forward with this? Are you going to be kind to me?" A rush of warm compassion for the man seated on her couch filled Alex's heart as she read the thoughts behind his inquiring eyes.

"Yes," she affirmed. "I think that's a very good sign."

The drive eased along, filled with conversation interspersed with silence and occasional bouts of jazz as Corey exposed Alex to his favorite CDs. Alex basked in the sensation of energized peace, of knowing she was entering uncharted territory, but with full awareness and joy. Cares and concerns slipped away as the wheels spun over miles of Michigan terrain. The metropolitan rush diminished into endless stretches of farmland edged in forests of pine and color-speckled trees holding onto the last remnants of their dried leaves.

They talked little of work. Rather, gentle probing questions were laid out to see how much the other was willing to share—questions about family, faith, personal conviction, and dreams yet unrealized. Each unfolding story assured Alex of her growing affection for this carefree and compassionate man who was allowing her into his life. Would they ever have connected if she had not asked him to dinner? She learned that Corey's parents and a married sister lived in Oregon. He had come to Michigan to attend college and never returned to the West Coast.

Being late in the season, the campground had few visitors. Corey chose a spot near a level meadow to pitch the tents, not far from the hiking trail. Lake Michigan lay less than a mile west, and the crisp autumn air rustled the branches and brushed a healthy glow across Alex's face. The pair investigated their surroundings and the first half-mile of the trail, searching for useable firewood before setting up the tents and enjoying a meal of sandwiches and fruit. Alex noted how carefully Corey disposed of the food wrappings.

"Leave it as you found it," he said. "That's the golden rule out here." The sun slipped behind the trees in a blaze of crimson, giving way to a turquoise sky dotted with emerging stars. The whispering breeze and birdsongs of earlier had ceased. Now the slow chirp of the last crickets of the season lulled from the meadow. Corey snapped the dry branches they had collected on the path into kindling and pulled a newspaper and a cord of split logs from the back of his SUV. Alex watched with interest as he crumpled sheets of newsprint, positioning them among the kindling, and rested the logs in a tepee shape over the whole affair. Rugged softness, that's how Corey seemed to her. He lit a match and the pile of wood and paper slowly surrendered into crackling flames.

"Where did you learn to do that?"

"My dad taught me how to build a campfire. He took my sister and me on a week-long camping trip every summer until I was seventeen. I had some of the best times of my childhood in the woods of Oregon."

"It sounds nice. Did your mother ever join you?"

"Occasionally. She preferred the time alone to visit her family and get the house back in order before her 'troops' returned."

Muted voices from adjacent campsites rose and fell in the darkness. Alex and Corey sat close to the glowing fire, hands clasped around mugs of strong coffee. The past few days had been warm for late October, but Alex was glad for the wool blanket thrown over her shoulders to fend off the night chill. Soft yellow firelight danced on their faces, its golden flicker bringing a tone of surrealism as the sky darkened. Alex pulled her eyes away from the mesmerizing fire to find Corey studying her face. He smiled gently at being caught.

"Are you enjoying yourself?" he asked.

"Yes, very much," Alex responded and leaned back in her folding chair. She turned back to the campfire; the smile left her face as she looked intently at the flickering light.

"Is something troubling you?" Corey asked.

"Oh, no," Alex laughed off the seriousness that had temporarily shrouded her. "I was just thinking, how beautiful this all is, how peaceful and simple. Yet it's so hard to pull away from the responsibilities of life to experience it. Life just takes over and crowds out whatever remnants of peace are left."

"It takes planning to make times like this happen. But it's worth it. When I lost Karen, I learned what is really important." Corey had not mentioned his former wife to Alex since those first pained months after the marriage fell apart and Alex didn't want him bringing her up now. Yes, Karen was gone, but she wondered how many memories still lingered in Corey's subconscious and if any longing remained.

"And what is that?" Alex questioned. Corey sighed and leaned back as he searched for the best words. Hands behind his head, he stared at the stars for several minutes as if pulling his thoughts from their still light.

"Finding those who are truly pivotal in your life—who genuinely know you and allow you to really know them, and to invest yourself in those people." He had emphasized the words *genuinely* and *really* as if they represented the crux of his intent.

"Like your kids," he continued. "There is a special relationship that you know will always be there."

"Not always," Alex protested. "Some people don't get along well with their children."

"That's true. But I think it's the exception. A decent parent will usually maintain a good relationship with their kids all their lives. That doesn't mean they will always be close by. But a strong bond holds up over distance."

"And, aside from your children, how do you determine who these people are?"

Corey leaned forward, studying the ground between his boots. "It's not easy. Spend time, become just vulnerable enough to see what they will do, see if you can trust them with more." He turned to give Alex a small smile. She wondered if he was sending her a subtle message. While she understood his meaning, she didn't wholly agree with his last statement. It often seemed to Alex those closest to a person were the most capable of hiding their true motives and intent, the most capable of causing pain.

"You married someone who you loved and felt you could trust. What happened with that?" She had asked out of curiosity, but the question sounded blunt and cruel in her ears. Corey looked at her, a hint of sadness clouding his eyes.

"I don't really know."

"I'm sorry, I didn't mean..."

"No, no, that's alright. It's a good question. One I have asked myself many times over the past two years. All I can say is, we never really *knew* each other." Alex silently pondered what Corey meant by that word 'knew'. He emphasized it like a mantra, like a deep magical word with hidden powers reserved for those chosen few who understood its spell. How well could one really know another person, anyway? Only by the outward telling of whatever they chose to share, and perhaps by common experiences. He continued, almost apologetically, his voice low over the slow chirp of crickets.

"I grew up in a remote area without much exposure to excitement. My first three years at U of M were pretty intense and without much of a social life. Then, in my senior year, I met Karen. She was the opposite of everything I came from. She was beautiful, worldly, and full of energy and new ideas. I was awestruck. She must have loved the way I doted on her. We were married two months after graduation. But I wasn't enough to keep her interested. Not for a lifetime." Corey poked at the dying fire with a stick as the logs shifted and crackled. "Enough about that. What about you, have you ever been married?"

Alex had anticipated this question. Though she didn't care for dredging up old failures, she knew the subject was inevitable.

"I was engaged once, during college," she began. She intended to drop it there, but Corey looked at her with intense eyes. "Brian and I hung out with a common group of friends. I had my eye on him for a while when slowly he began to take a more serious interest in me. I was anxious to get married; I probably pushed too hard."

"So, what happened?"

"A few weeks before the wedding date, I found him at a restaurant with a pretty medical student. They were enjoying more than the meal."

"Wow, what a letdown."

"When I questioned him the next day, he told me he had been seeing her for months and intended to keep doing so after we were married." Corey snorted and shook his head. "Needless to say, I never walked down the aisle. We didn't want the same type of relationship. I'm thankful now that I never went through with it."

The two sat in silent solidarity until the fire dimmed to an orange glow beneath the charred logs.

"We'd better hit the sack so we can get an early start tomorrow," Corey said as he stretched and rose from his chair. "I'll wake you for breakfast." He stood over Alex and looked down into her sleepy eyes framed with wisps of hair that had come loose from her ponytail. As she gave him a slight smile, he reached out, cupping her cheek in his hand. Alex welcomed the touch, closing her eyes and leaning her face into his gentle hand. His hand warmed her face, but what enthralled her was the warmth that flooded her heart in response to his simple, tender gesture.

Alex awoke the next morning to the cooing of a mourning dove calling across the meadow. Such a sad and beautiful song, reminiscent of a cello, the first note strong and rich followed by two or three softer tones. She listened to the melody as if for the first time, enjoying each note. As the daze of sleep lifted, she noticed the pleasant chirp of cardinals and chickadees filling in the top notes. Not since she was a child had she felt such eagerness for a completely unstructured day. She had no idea what was in store, and the exhilaration of unknown adventure was wonderful. Alex felt like a little girl on Christmas morning, waiting anxiously for her parents to wake up so the festivities could begin.

She lay in silence within her small, borrowed tent until she heard the rustling and zipping of Corey exiting his sleeping bag. She stifled a laugh after hearing a crash of aluminum cooking equipment followed by a muffled, "shhhh." Peeking through the top inch of open zipper in her tent, she spotted Corey walking toward the trail. Quickly, she kicked off her sleeping bag and pulled on her jeans. Getting dressed in such close quarters certainly was a challenge. She wanted to shower and brush her teeth before greeting Corey. Thank heaven the campground had modern bathroom facilities.

Walking back to the field with damp hair wisped about her forehead, Alex found Corey busily organizing their little campsite.

"Good morning," he shouted as she approached.

She laughed at the excitement in his voice.

"Same to you," she hollered back. "What's for breakfast?"

"We're keeping it simple this morning." He put a protein bar and a banana in her hand as she approached the tent. Alex wondered how quickly this breakfast would be burned off with hiking all day.

"Oh, I have more for the backpack. Bagels, carrots, fruit, water, we're all set."

"Do you realize you just read my mind?" Alex remarked.

"Really?"

"Yes! I was thinking how hungry we'll be in about two hours on this breakfast, and you answered just as if I had said it out loud."

" Hmm, how about that. We must think alike." Corey put the pack on his back and added a camera around his neck. "Are you ready?"

"Don't you need to use the facilities or brush your teeth?" Alex asked. Corey grinned at her.

"Already did. I was up at six o'clock, then came back to my tent to read for awhile until you woke up." Alex blushed at what Corey must be thinking.

"I was never a morning person."

"That's okay. With all the walking you'll get in today, it's good that you're rested." Corey shifted his backpack to a more comfortable position and turned toward the open meadow. "Just follow me, and let me know if you need anything," Corey told her. They started across the field in the direction of the lake.

Though the sky held some clouds and the air was brisk, Alex felt comfortable with the layered clothing Corey had suggested. Alex hoped her hair would dry quickly; the morning breeze made her head cold. Corey stopped in his tracks and spun around.

"I almost forgot the most important essential. Wait here." He jogged back to the tent and disappeared inside. Moments later, Corey emerged with a brown leather panama hat and proudly handed it to Alex.

"What's this?"

"I bought this for you to add to your collection, except you have to wear this one." It was a sharp-looking hat made of softly brushed leather the color of bittersweet chocolate, sporting a beaded drawstring to keep it in place.

"Oh, you shouldn't have done…" Corey grabbed the hat from her hand and plopped it on her head.

"There. It looks great."

Alex laughed. He had read her mind again, and he was so excited about his special gift, she had no choice but to accept. They tromped off into the trees like two children seeking hidden treasure.

The trail wound through several miles of woodlands. Alex saw plants she had never seen before and heard unfamiliar birds that must never venture to the east side of the state. She reveled in her sense of innocent discovery. Beech and maple trees hovered above; at times their branches groaned and creaked as they held back the lake winds. Dried leaves, brown but still holding bits of gold, crimson, and wine, adorned the forest floor and crumpled loudly under foot. Small un-seen creatures scampered through the leaves as the hikers approached. Alex marveled at the life surrounding her. Even the stately trees seemed animated.

Among the fading leaves and bare branches, Corey pointed to a cluster of evergreen trees lining the side of the trail.

"Go stand over there," he instructed Alex. "Back up. Get right next to the branches." She did as he suggested. "Now inhale." Alex took a deep breath and closed her eyes, allowing the thick, sweet scent of balsam to settle into her chest.

"Gotcha," Corey said as he snapped her picture.

"It smells like Christmas!" she exclaimed, re-membering the live trees that had adorned her child-hood home.

Corey led them to a narrow trail that rose decid-edly uphill. The trees began to thin as the trail spilled out to a sandy knoll overlooking the Lake Michigan shore. Alex gasped as they approached the expanse of blue water, the waves below splashing and running to settle on the sandy shore that seemed to stretch for eternity, dotted occasionally with boulders skirted with white crests.

"It's beautiful!"

"So, was this worth trekking four miles in the woods?"

"Oh, yes. Actually, I enjoyed the woods."

"This is a great spot. Hang gliders use it as a launch site."

A gust tugged at Alex's hat, threatening to cast it off her head and down the knoll into the water. She grabbed it just in time. "A bit breezy up here, isn't it?"

"Here." Corey took the drawstring in hand and slid the wooden bead up to just under her chin. They stood, looking into each other's face and Alex felt a surge of delight at his closeness—at the softness of his eyes and the brush of his fingers along her chin. All at once his face came closer and he was kissing her lips, gingerly at first and then, gradually, with more passion. She took his head in her hands and kissed back, reveling in the full awaking of what had silently lain beneath consciousness for the past two years: the fact that she was in love with Corey Foster.

Chapter seven

Subtly, Alex shifted her thoughts of a relationship with Corey from guarded hope to anticipatory interest. The wall of uncertainty had been demolished. Both were certain of the other's interest in moving toward a more intimate relationship, yet Alex preferred a slow progression. A weekend fling wasn't on her agenda. She longed more for a deep friendship. There was certainly potential. Their spontaneous kiss had created a relaxed enjoyment of one another— more touches were given, longer looks were shared. On Sunday morning, Alex looked forward to the day ahead as they packed the camping gear.

"Where are we going today?" she asked.

"It's a surprise."

"Really? Will I like it?"

"Oh, I'd say so." Corey pulled a leaflet from his pack and waved it toward Alex. "Ever been here?" She grabbed the glossy brochure and looked at the cover. SAUGATUCK / DOUGLAS stared back at her.

"No, can't say I have."

"Well, from what I know about your tastes for poking around in unique shops and galleries, this should really earn me some brownie points." Alex thought his points were considerably high already, but was intrigued that he would arrange a day that she would enjoy.

Saugatuck and its neighbor Douglas were the sorts of towns Alex may have dreamed of but thought could not exist in reality. Victorian beauty was mixed with an eclectic array of shops and art galleries bursting with unique treasures. Quaint nooks held collections of paintings, glasswork, Indian rugs, pottery, and jewelry. Alex and Corey walked hand-in-hand along a dockside street lined with historic buildings and tempting shops beckoning them inside. October breezes lulled over softly splashing waves in the harbor, then came ashore, carrying scents of culinary delights that spilled from restaurant doorways.

"As impressive as these crafts are, I have no desire to own a boat." Corey remarked, looking out at the waterfront.

"You don't like the water?"

"No, I wouldn't want the upkeep! And think how much time is spent coming up with a name." He moved toward tethered sailboats and yachts gently bobbing in unison.

"'My Desire,' 'Stress-Buster,' 'Sin-or-swim'... what kind of name is that?" He playfully tugged at Alex's arm and feigned tossing her into the harbor as she laughed in delight.

"I LOVE this place!" Alex exclaimed as they stood close. "And I love you," she said, embracing Corey in a warm hug. The words slipped past the censor of reason and spilled out of her as naturally as breathing. He chuckled at her enthusiasm, his eyes laughing in her happiness. But he did not reiterate her sentiment. The words, "I love you, too" did not come. Alex brushed away the vacancy of his silence. *Stupid. I should have kept my feelings to myself.*

The pair sauntered through the town, sampling wine, commenting on each other's tastes in art, and stopping for dinner in a busy café. As the sun sank toward Lake Michigan, the sidewalks became less populated, and shop owners gradually slipped 'Closed' signs in their windows.

"We'd better head back," Alex said, noting the time. Corey looked at his watch and shrugged.

"Can you miss work tomorrow?"

"Well, I shouldn't. But I don't have any appoint-ments scheduled." Frankly, Alex preferred to extend her time with Corey as long as possible, even if it meant missing work the next day.

"I did make arrangements at one of the inns, just in case we were having too much fun to leave." Corey flashed a smile her way. Alex looked a bit perplexed.

"We do have separate rooms," he continued teasingly.

"Oh, I wasn't thinking about that," Alex lied. They walked in silence for a few more minutes. A gentle moistness hung in the air. "It's starting to rain." She turned and looked down the street at the colorful storefronts, soft yellow radiance spilling from their windows into the dimming twilight.

She didn't want the day to end. Not yet. "All right," Alex said, "let's leave tomorrow morning."

As they walked to the car, the rain intensified until it became a downpour. Alex shrieked in delight and ran under a nearby awning for protection, Corey following after. They stood shivering as daylight surrendered its last vestige of warmth to darkness. Alex peered in the shop window at an array of curiosities until her eyes fell on an unusual piece in the corner, a doll's bed covered with a pastel quilt and a stuffed animal curled up on it. All at once the "stuffed" animal moved.

"Look!" Alex pointed. "It's real." The object of her interest was a marmalade cat, comfortably curled on what must have been his personal bed. The sign on the door said the shop was open for another ten minutes, and Alex had to meet the cat in person. A brass bell chimed upon entering the cozy shop. Fragrant lavender, rose, and freesia welcomed them inside. Unfortunately, the cat was more interested in sleep than in meeting another customer.

"That's Sam," said an elderly woman emerging from behind the counter. "He's been with me for fifteen years. Keeps the place in order when I'm not here." At hearing his name, Sam rose and stretched, allowing Alex to lift him gently and hold him close. She cradled the sleepy cat as one would a baby and cooed until a muffled purr emanated from his chest.

"How sweet. I have a cat myself; I don't know what I'd do without him."

"Are you folks from the area?"

"No, we live near Detroit."

"Ah. We get a lot of folks from the Detroit area in the summer months. It's slowed down quite a bit now. Did you happen to catch our Halloween Festival on Saturday? Now that was a fun time. I've never seen so many unique costumes as I did during the parade this year."

"No, we've just arrived today." While the two women chatted, Corey had moved into the shop and was looking intently in a glass case.

"Would you like to see something in the case?" the proprietor asked.

"Yes, I would, " he replied. Alex, curious about what could have piqued his interest after a full day of browsing, returned Sam to his bed and approached the counter. Within the case lay several pieces of handcrafted jewelry. Elegant rings, earrings, and necklaces made from gold and silver, some with semi-precious stones, gleamed under the glass.

"This is a new artist to the area," the older woman commented. "I've just begun to carry her items and they are selling wonderfully. She has such exclusive style." Alex never would have anticipated that Corey would be interested in jewelry. Perhaps he's found something his mother would like for Christmas. He pointed to a gold heart pendant with a delicate leaf pattern etched on its surface. From the base of the heart dangled a small emerald-cut citrine, the color of golden maple leaves splashed with sunshine. The shop owner lifted the necklace from the case and placed it in Corey's waiting hand.

"This is a lovely piece. The heart is actually a locket," she explained.

"Do you like it?" Corey asked, handing the piece to Alex.

"It's beautiful, and very unique. Who is it for?" Corey stepped back and looked at her, surprise on his face.

"Well, for you, of course!"

"For me? Really!" At first she was flattered and then she felt awkward. "Oh, that's not necessary. Really," and she handed the necklace back to him.

"No," Corey protested, putting his hand over hers, "I want you to have it. It's a memento of the weekend. Besides, it will look nice on you." He took the necklace and clasped it around her neck. Gold and citrine sparkled against her cream sweater. Turning to the smiling woman behind the counter, Corey confirmed, "We'll take it."

Alex fingered the treasure around her neck as the shopkeeper left to fetch a box for safekeeping.

"Well, thank you. I will treasure it." She flushed

at Corey's thoughtfulness, not accustomed to such special treatment. She would have to take a picture of him to put in the locket. No, better wait on that. She could see the women at Barringer having a field day with that one. She would think of something else to keep within the locket that would remind her of Corey, and of this wonderful place.

They didn't have to travel far to reach their accommodations. Corey had selected an elegant inn tucked along a winding street and only steps from the Lake Michigan shoreline. Alex waited in the common area watching the glow of a crackling fire cast delicate shadows along vintage furnishings, resting in the comfort she felt with Corey. He was easy to spend time with. As she fondled the golden heart around her throat, she wondered how deeply into his life she would be allowed.

"All set." Corey stood at her side extending a brass room key. She remembered the last time a man had handed her a room key and felt even more grateful for her choice on that evening.

How ironic. Now the man toward whom she felt undeniable love was handing her a key to her own room. "You're in room number 12." They climbed the staircase to the appointed rooms and he stopped at her door. "I'm right next door in room 10. Just holler if you need anything."

"Great. See you in the morning?" she asked with a slight smile.

"Yep. How about if I meet you downstairs at

eight for breakfast before heading out?"

Alex turned the key in its lock to enter her room when Corey set his duffel bag on the floor and gave her a soft hug. "I had a great time," he whispered. Alex struggled as the words she so wanted to say stuck in her throat. Wanting to invite him to her room, but preferring that he make the first move, she said simply, "So did I." They released their embrace and she entered her room.

Showered and in her silk pajamas, Alex lay on the bed and pulled the covers over her shoulders. Moonlight streamed in the window and nestled on the bed beside her. All she could think of was the man in the next room. Was he sleeping? Could he be thinking about her? Why couldn't he say, "I love you, too," when it was clear he had feelings for her? Perhaps he needed more time. It seemed crazy to lay awake in the darkness when such a wonderful man lay just a few yards away. Alex felt drawn to Corey's presence. She yearned to lie next to him, to feel the touch of his hands in her hair, to hear his melting voice. She couldn't pinpoint what held her back from inviting him to her room. Perhaps it would be all right to visit him. Then she could leave if she had made a bad decision. Slowly, she pulled back the covers and slipped her legs over the side of the bed. His presence in the next room was stronger than her reserve, and she found herself walking into the hallway. She padded to his door and gently rapped, praying he would not think her a complete idiot. The door opened slightly, and then Corey opened it further as he saw Alex standing before him in her butter-yellow pajamas. His eyes smiled, but then a concerned look crossed his face.

"Is anything wrong? Do you need something?" he asked.

Alex took a deep breath before responding. "I need you."

A look that combined tenderness with pain washed over Corey's face and Alex studied his eyes carefully for a response. He reached through the door and slowly took her hand.

"Come on, come on in." Inside a fireplace glowed with warmth and soft light. "I asked for a fireplace, in case…" Corey couldn't finish, as Alex took his face in her hands and kissed him, a man who would respect her enough to let her choose the time when she would give herself to him. Her heart swelled with desire and love as they made their way toward the Victorian four-poster bed. They made love, bodies caressing in tender discovery, and then lay entwined in each other's arms until overcome with sleep.

The beach was empty on this chill autumn morning as Corey and Alex bounded down rustic wooden steps twisting toward the shoreline. They struggled to keep their balance on the mounded pale sand, laughing and tugging each other toward the blue water. Rhythmic waves splashed playfully where the pair walked, their bodies gently bumping as the sand shifted underfoot. They walked a long while, enjoying the music offered up from Lake Michigan: a steady drone of waves punctuated with gulls calling across the water.

The vastness of Lake Michigan brought them to reflective silence as they walked along the shoreline. The scene around them demanded respect, as if this moment in time had been ordained since another lifetime. *The shoreline makes one ponder life's purpose, to question what should have been accomplished and what is yet to be done,* Alex mused. A unique energy arose from the waves, bathing their souls in introspection. *What is the purpose of my life? Have I taken the best direction so far?* Alex's thoughts rolled and receded with the waves, and she felt a part of her linger behind, transfixed by the lake's magic, even as she and Corey slowly climbed the steps back toward the road. She hated the thought of leaving this place, of returning to the ritual of daily life at Barringer. Yet she would be returning with the precious gift of Corey's affection, a gift that would add comfort and excitement to her days.

"Guess what day this is?" Corey remarked as they reached the top.

"Uh, Monday?"

"Besides that."

"Oh! Halloween!"

"Right, and you have to come to the midnight bonfire," he said. Alex looked confused. "My neighborhood has a celebratory bonfire in the park on Halloween night," Corey continued. "It's a blast!"

Alex envisioned a bunch of college kids hanging around drinking beer and poking sticks into a campfire, but she felt it appropriate to humor him. "Sure, sounds like fun."

The "campfire" Alex had envisioned was far from the actual spectacle now before her. Sundry combustible wood items including logs, crates, scraps, a retired door or two, window frames, a dilapidated chair and a number of split two-by-fours had been donated to the cause. The pile reached as high as her bungalow and almost covered an equal space. Streets lined with quaint homes bordered the small park where the pile stood. Jack-o'-lanterns dotting several porches lent their mysterious glow to the night. Children in costumes chased each other and tumbled down a small hillside, energized from house-to-house canvassing and too much sugar. Alex laughed as a little boy darted about in a jester's hat, bells jingling from the tips of multi-colored curved points protruding from his head.

Winding through clusters of neighbors, Alex heard snatches of discussion dotted with giggling teenage banter as she stepped up to the yellow tape surrounding the sacrificial pile. Words lifted in the darkness.

"So, he got three A's and two B's?"

91

"Are you voting on the school millage proposal?"

"Mindy, stay close to Mommy."

"I think he's soooooo cute!"

"No way! The Chargers are a better team than the Patriots, hands down."

How often, Alex wondered, might these neighbors leave the sanctuary of their homes, soft blue light from the television glowing, to share friendly conversation with those who existed in such close proximity?

"Come on, Mr. Firelighter, light my fire!" a man yelled into the night. Slowly, others joined in until the entire park was shouting in unison.

"You'll want to move back a bit," Corey stepped up from behind and handed Alex a plastic cup brimming with apple cider. "It gets a *little* warm." A young man dressed in a long black cape approached the pile, lighted torch in hand. He lifted the torch above him and swung around to face the crowd.

"Come on, Mr. Firelighter, light my fire!"

Wild cheers erupted as he turned and threw the torch into the mountainous fodder. Alex smiled as she caught sight of the police officer in uniform under the black robe. Slowly at first the cardboard boxes and scrap wood at the base caught fire. Within minutes the mountain was ablaze, a river of crackling yellow-orange flames flowing upward into the dark night. The crowd released a spontaneous murmur of awe and broke into applause. Spectators were forced to move back as sparks flew and charred bits of paper rained down from the airborne smoke gathering above the flames.

"It's incredible!" Alex shouted at Corey over the crackling fire. "I've never seen anything like it." The heat intensified until it was no longer bearable to stay put.

Bright as daylight near the blaze, the faces further beyond were illuminated with a warm glow. Alex enjoyed the happy energy of those around her, the pleasant faces nodding in friendly welcome as she followed Corey away from the fire. They stood holding each other close, watching the fire until the crowd slowly began to disperse. Where Alex had first stood admiring the blaze, yellow tape had stretched and melted from the heat and now lay in a wilted strand along the grass.

Chapter Eight

*N*ever *have a romantic relationship with someone from work.* Where had she heard that before? As November unfolded and Alex labored over Tri-Plex and several other client projects, it was difficult not to stop by Corey's office daily for a respite. Alex enjoyed occasional breaks when Corey would appear at her office door bearing a cup of hot tea. Tender smiles and sideways glances were traded during staff meetings. Yet the two were discrete, and no one seemed to notice the special bond that had grown between them. Alex often fondled the locket around her neck, contemplating their special secret. She made a point not to divulge their relationship during business hours. Tuesday evenings were reserved for dinner at Alex's home while Corey treated to dinner out on Fridays. Only Sue Duprey knew the two were seeing each other on a more personal basis.

Life at Barringer was complicated enough. Alex was determined to keep low-key about her denied promotion, waiting to see what the first quarter would bring. Perhaps, once the Rossman account was secured and Riley returned, things would settle down a bit. Then, she would pursue her status again with Seaton. Right now, her days were full with the Tri-Plex acquisition and other projects. John Tierney had finally unpacked his office. A cool formality hung in the air between him and Alex when they were forced to speak. Alex wondered if a move to John's team was worth striving for. While potential for more salary was evident, so was the prospect of working day after day with a man for whom she had no respect.

"Kate Rossman has accused you of trying to take her position," Sue shared with Alex over lunch.

"That's ludicrous," Alex responded. "I don't want her job; I just want what was promised to me. I don't see why we both can't work on the larger accounts."

"She probably heard Tierney's version of the story. He had to come up with some excuse for his tantrum. John wants to make you the bad guy. How else can you explain it?"

"So is he any closer to acquiring Rossman, Kidwell and Sparks? Has my sacrificial offering brought any money to the firm?"

"Not yet. He has a meeting scheduled just after the holidays."

"Why so late?"

Sue just shrugged. "Actually, Barringer's timing

was perfect in hiring Kate; Rossman is looking to acquire several law offices nationally over the next few years. Kate isn't doing much right now. She'll be working with John exclusively on the law firm if they win the business."

"Amazing. So Kate Rossman gets hired to act as bait for her husband's law firm while I am honored with a title."

"That's about how it is."

"So, is everyone in the office talking about what a bitch I am?"

Sue chuckled. "Only the important ones." Alex sipped on hot tea, warmth oozing from the ceramic mug to caress her fingers. She loved the feel of a warm mug in her hands. It brought comfort in times of stress. She again pondered John Tierney's reaction to her potential transfer to his team and his warped sense of how it might interrupt his plans. More disturbing was that Seaton accommodated him.

"You know," Alex said, "Until recently I never realized how partial Barringer is to its male employees. I suppose I didn't want to see it, especially since everything has always gone so well."

"You weren't in a position to notice until recently. Riley probably protected you from the reality of it."

"Reality. Amazing how perception changes it. So what's actually real?"

"The fact that the male consultants make about $25,000 a year more than you do. Now that's reality for you!" Sue huffed.

Alex set down her mug and dropped her jaw in disbelief. "How do you know?"

"Human Resources accidentally left a compensation report on the copier—I just happened to find it."

"Why didn't you tell me?"

Sue shrugged, "I didn't want to get you worked up. What would be the point?"

Alex leaned into the table to look into her friend's blue eyes. "Do you know what Kate is making?" she whispered.

Sue shook her head. "It was before she came."

Alex closed her eyes and took a long, deep breath to slow the blood that raced to her temples. She had tried to fend it off for months, but the favorable perceptions of her long-time employer were being progressively, definitively weakened. She could never return to the place from which she came. This was right up there with losing one's virginity.

"Here's another example for you," Sue had fished her memory and was pleased to bring in another catch. "The all male-golf outing!"

"That's right!" Alex remembered. Every summer Seaton hosted a consultant and client golf outing up north, no women allowed. Since Alex didn't golf, it never mattered much to her. Now she saw the blatant disparity of it.

Sue continued, "Women are so conditioned to expect less, we aren't surprised when it happens."

"Well, perhaps it's time to set a precedent to change that!" Alex remarked. But even as she uttered them, the words sounded hollow. Who was she to tout the flag of girl power? Hadn't she just swallowed the ultimatum of staying put and out of the way? What could she do to change it? Absolutely nothing. She could leave, but that would only be admitting defeat. Who would be winning then? Not her. Alex wasn't ready to lose the one last part of her that she held so closely to her heart, the part that made up the person she had grown into, her career. The long days were a welcome diversion, an avoidance of a dark and quiet house devoid of dinner warming for the family or the shrill voices of children arguing over the TV remote. Barringer was all she had, after all.

Five messages! What could so many people want during lunch hour? Alex made notes as she listened to each caller. The last message had a tone of urgency.

"Alex, it's Amanda at Tri-Plex. Please call me right away." Usually, such callers needed a quick answer or a routine issue handled. Alex was particularly sensitive to her newest account and returned that call first.

"Hi, Amanda, it's me."

"Hi, Alex. I'll get right to it. We've heard that Barringer is going under and are a little concerned about your ability to carry through with our contract." Alex's heart stopped.

"Where did you hear this?"

"There is a press release floating around. One of

the guys in acquisitions saw it posted on your competitor's web site." Alex stammered through her response.

"I...I know nothing about this. Can you tell me the Web site so I can read a copy?" After assuring Amanda that Barringer was alive and well, Alex entered the site and found the release. She sent it to the printer and raced to pick it up. It could be disastrous if word got out this way. She would let Seaton know so he could control how the employees found out. Quietly shutting her office door behind her, she stood and scanned the release. The article was brief, only one page.

Proposed Sale of Barringer Consulting Group

..... the current owners of Barringer Consulting Group, a leading Detroit firm offering corporate merger and acquisition consultation, announced yesterday that they have entered into an agreement to sell Barringer to the law firm of Rossman, Kidwell And Sparks for a sum of $25 million. A failing profit margin at Barringer triggered the transaction.

Alex fumbled for her chair and plopped into it. Rossman! That would explain Kate's presence. But why would Barringer hire Kate Rossman if her husband's firm planned to take over the company—to get inside information? Had Seaton known about this all along? She read on.

Wade Sparks, Managing Partner, said, "Barringer offers some excellent consultants. The union will bring us specialized expertise in the area of corporate acquisition that is currently not available. As we strive to offer a single resource for all our clients' needs, we look forward to the opportunities presented in our acquisition of Barringer."

Rossman, Kidwell and Sparks is the largest law firm in the Midwest with 320 attorneys and additional offices located in Florida and Washington. Its clients include many of the largest corporations across the nation. An aggressive acquisition strategy is planned over the next four years to develop a more national presence.

Alex, stunned, stared out her office windows at the dove-gray sky, trying to process the facts as swells of unwelcome anxiety rose in her chest. Amanda had exaggerated the situation. Going under was not the same as being acquired. Yet questions raced in a confusing jumble while her intellect tried to answer them.

Why had Seaton thrown a party celebrating their successful year if the results were so poor? Was it to lull everyone into a false sense of security? To further impress upon Kate Rossman and her important husband that Barringer was worth seizure? What was Kate's real role here? That was a question with no clear answer. Perhaps she was hired to collect inside information on Barringer's clients and prospects, or on the employees. Under the guise that Barringer had been seeking her husband's law firm as a client, no one would suspect that Barringer was actually the one to be acquired. Could Kate be stalling the process of Barringer working on the law firm's acquisition project that Sue had mentioned at lunch? Why should Rossman contract with Barringer and pay a hefty consulting fee when they could control the process in-house once the acquisition of Barringer was final?

Slowly, Alex lifted the telephone and called Seaton's extension.

"Do you have a few minutes? There's something I want to show you." She tried to sound calm and pleasant.

"Sure, Alex, come on in."

She entered Seaton's office to find him intently working through several piles of documents spread across his great desk. He looked at her blankly as she quietly shut the door and handed him the press release.

"I thought you should see this before anyone else in the office gets word." As he read the paper in front of him, his lips pursed and then he let out a deep sigh.

"Where did you get this?"

"Amanda at Tri-Plex brought it to my attention. They found it on the Clark web site." Charles swiveled to his credenza and filed the paper within the myriad folders hanging there. Alex noted that the particular folder where he filed the release contained several inches of paperwork and wondered what other tidbits of information the folder held.

"Has anyone else seen it?"

"I don't know. I don't think so."

"That's good, because it's complete hogwash."

Alex was surprised at his comment. How could a press release be hogwash? "But they've quoted Wade Sparks," she argued.

"I knew this might come up," Seaton assured. "The law firm has talked about putting out the word of our purchase to help them acquire some crucial clients and to set the tone for the acquisitions to come. In reality, we are poised to develop a strategic partnership with Rossman, Kidwell and Sparks to help them acquire many, many smaller firms across the country. The process has actually begun and will be under way by the end of the first quarter. They will not be buying us out." Alex thought about Seaton's explanation carefully. It sounded reasonable enough, but then she didn't have all the facts, either. All she could do was take Seaton at his word.

"But won't this hurt our position with our clients? Tri-Plex thinks we're going under. And I'm sure our competition is using this news against us."

"It could, but only temporarily. As soon as all the issues are ironed out between Barringer and Rossman, a new release will be issued rescinding the offer to purchase." He rose from his chair, a signal for her to leave, and walked her toward the door.

"I would appreciate it if you wouldn't share this with anyone just yet," he said. "I'll pull together a meeting in the next few days to address the staff and advise how we should respond to our clients. Let me know if you have any more questions." Alex nodded her agreement and opened the door.

"Alex," Seaton's voice commanded that she stop in the doorway, "thanks for bringing it here first."

Chapter Nine

Alex stood before the elevator eagerly waiting for her Lazarus to emerge, the one who would make Barringer as it had been, would make things right again. The doors slid open slowly.

"Riley, you can't imagine how glad I am to see you," Alex said, giving a quick hug to her old friend as he stepped off the elevator. "The place just hasn't been the same."

"Well, it's good to be back in the game."

Alex followed Riley like an excited pup as he found his way to his office amidst handshakes and back-pats and occasional shouts over cubicle walls of, "Hey, old man, glad you're back," and "Gee, I thought you'd retire after all that."

They entered the sanctum of his office—full of mahogany bookcases, brown leather, and a half-dead ficus tree. A cobalt-blue vase sparkled in the morning sun, filled to capacity with roses the color of

Devonshire cream—a welcome-back gift from Alex. He did look rested, younger, with wisps of white hair falling over his tanned forehead and a brightness in his eyes that had been lacking months before.

Only a week earlier Charles had convened an employee meeting to explain the incident of the press release.

"We are not being bought," his booming voice reassured. "No one need fear for their position. Our partnership with Rossman, Kidwell and Sparks will catapult our firm into greater success and prosperity." Riley had sat quietly in that meeting, preparing for his return to duty.

"I'm sure you have a lot of catching up to do," Alex said, "so I'll leave you alone. But you have to leave lunch open. How does the Bistro sound?"

"That works for me."

Alex thought it odd that Seaton and John Tierney had not snagged Riley for lunch on his first day back. Just as well. She would enjoy visiting with her old friend and filling him in on all the Barringer happenings since his departure.

"Alex," Riley's voice caught her in the door, "thanks."

"Any time. Glad you're back."

It was Monday. Thanksgiving was just three days away, and Alex's thoughts were focused on seeing her family. She loved Thanksgiving more than any other holiday. It offered an unpretentious coziness that allowed her to nest in a warm home with family, savoring the scent of seasoned turkey and dressing, anticipating billows of whipped cream on clove-spiced pumpkin pie. She appreciated an uncomplicated holiday without the need for gift-giving and decorating, not needing to be anywhere or do anything but visit—an art she felt was lost to modern life.

Alex had asked Corey to join her for dinner. He had seemed happy for the invitation, but explained that he and the boys would be visiting his parents in Oregon and would not return until Sunday. Alex was only mildly disappointed at first, but became more so as the holiday approached. Corey had become a friend and occasional lover. Though only a month since the camping trip, his presence in her daily life had become very important to her. She was glad to have made the first step in their relationship, to have surrendered her complacency to pursue Corey's affections. Alex felt Corey was a comfortable companion, easy to talk with, easy to listen to, and she enjoyed the expectancy of many happy experiences together as their relationship matured.

The Bistro was quieter than usual, probably due to the regulars taking the week off for the holiday. Alex and Riley took a booth toward the back.

"Congratulations, again, on getting the Tri-Plex account. Good work," Riley began.

"Thanks, but it almost wasn't worth the price of getting it."

Riley raised an eyebrow. "Meaning what?"

"Remember Dennis Mitchell? Let's just say he wanted more than a firm handshake to close the deal." Riley took a moment to catch her meaning and then burst into abrupt laughter, sobered, and looked at Alex with a fatherly eye.

"Oh, don't worry, he didn't get his way."

"I'm relieved to hear it." They ordered comfort food, bowls of steaming cheese broccoli soup with thick croutons on top.

"Though John Tierney did. Do you know he actually packed up his office and threatened to leave because I pursued the promotion to his team?"

Riley shook his head. "Tierney's got an agenda all his own, warped as it may be." Riley quieted as he ate, and Alex could tell he was contemplating something. "What do you think of this buyout business?"

"I'm not sure," Alex answered slowly. "There's something going on under the surface. I just haven't determined what it is yet. Somehow I don't quite trust what Seaton's feeding us."

"Hmmm." Riley pushed his soup bowl aside and rested his hands on the spot where it had been, his fingers entwined, lightly opened, and then entwined again.

"What's on your mind?" Alex asked.

"I did a lot of thinking while recuperating from surgery. Almost dying does that to you. And, I've been watching what is going on with Barringer. I don't necessarily want to be a part of it any longer."

"You're leaving?"

Riley nodded sheepishly. Alex felt an empty sensation in the pit of her stomach. "Will you retire?"

"No, I'm not ready for that yet. Actually, I have a better idea." Riley leaned into the table, his eyes as bright as a child's on Christmas morning. "I'm branching out, setting up my own firm."

"No kidding?" Alex eyed Riley with surprise and awe. While it sounded simple enough, Alex knew becoming self-employed could be fraught with complexities.

"How will you establish your client base?"

"I'll purchase my clients from Barringer and take them with me."

"What if they won't sell?"

"They've done it before. They'll sell. If not, the clients will move anyway. I've already talked to them and they're ready to follow. I've consulted an attorney about Barringer's non-compete contract; he says it won't hold up in court because they've breached it several times with other former employees."

"When will this happen?"

"Not for a few more months. There's a loan pending with the bank, and I've been looking at office space to lease. In the meantime, you can't breathe a word of this to anyone."

"Don't worry," Alex assured. She then thought of the compromising situation Riley had just put her in with her employer. "Why are you telling me this?"

"I want to take you with me."

"Really?"

"Sure. Between your accounts and mine we would be set. And I could pay you more than what you would have made on Tierney's team."

Alex fell silent. It did sound like an intriguing offer. Still, it was a bit frightening leaving the security of a national consulting firm to join a start-up that might fail as easily as succeed. Yet Riley was right about the quality of the accounts, and there would be more control. Besides, she liked the idea of her future resting in Riley's hands as opposed to Seaton and his "We are not being bought" story. Still, if things worked out at Barringer, she did have many years and a good reputation invested there. Riley sensed the conflict in her mind.

"I know it's a risk, but everything worthwhile is," Riley assured her. "You need to think long and hard about where you are going to end up if you stay put. If there ever was a good old boy's club, Barringer is it."

"Do you really think I would be held back because of my gender? That's so outdated and incomprehensible."

Riley smirked in response. "There is a very small male 'in' crowd that you will never break into. The more successful you become and the harder you try to penetrate its walls, the stronger the resistance will be to keep you out. You don't see it because you are so enmeshed."

"Why aren't you in it?"

"Because I chose not to be." The waitress interrupted with an offer of dessert and Riley accepted with an order for pecan pie, insisting that Alex share in the pleasure. They ate dessert in brief silence, each in their own thoughts.

"Have you ever seen the movie 'Gaslight'?" Riley asked.

"No. Isn't that an older flick?"

"It's from the 1940s, but you might find it interesting. You should watch it this weekend." He pointed his fork at her for emphasis and a piece of pecan flew off and landed in Alex's hair, sending them both into restrained laughter. A matronly lady frowned from the adjacent booth and shook her head. Alex leaned toward her .

"It's okay, we work together." She picked the sticky nut from her hair and looked at Riley quizzically. "Would you bring anyone else?"

"I've thought about making an offer to Parker."

"Parker?" Alex couldn't hide her surprise. "Why him?"

"I know you don't think much of Parker, but he has a lot of potential and a lot of energy. I'll need someone to go after new accounts while you and I are handling the existing clients."

"Have you told him yet?"

"No. I have a breakfast meeting with him this Friday to share the news." Riley sat back and studied Alex's face for signs of acceptance. Her smile caused him to quietly nod, as if they had just entered into an unspoken contract.

"Go ahead and think about it over the holiday. I

know it's a lot to swallow right now and there will be many details to talk about over the next few months."

"No, it's just….you took me a bit by surprise. I'll think it over and let you know if I have more questions next week."

Alex pondered Riley's offer throughout the next day and up to Wednesday evening. Her quiet kitchen allowed her to think over her response as she mixed pumpkin pie filling and gathered the ingredients for the Boston cream pie. She struggled to convince her logic, to turn off the critical inner voice that preferred the known, liked security and a certain tired sameness. She could not remember a time before Barringer. The thought of leaving frightened her, yet in her heart Alex knew that taking the risk and leaving with Riley was the right thing to do. It was difficult, but appropriate.

Alex touched the doorbell, a Boston cream pie resting on one arm and a pumpkin pie on the other. Tiny snowflakes intermittently flecked the air, a warning of an early winter season. The door flew open to reveal an excited five-year-old.

"Aunt Ali! Aunt Ali's here!" When Sarah was a toddler, she had problems pronouncing the "x" in Alex. Alex had become 'Ali', and the pet name had stuck. Alex carefully balanced the pies and laughed as Sarah's arms wrapped around her legs in a tight hug. Amber entered the foyer and rescued the Boston cream pie.

"Good to see you," said Amber, pecking Alex's cheek in a quick greeting. "Oh, look, Sarah! Boston cream, your very favorite." Sarah smiled up at Alex, a single admiration society. Alex knew Sarah loved her, even after months of absence. It was as if all of the sisterly admiration and love Amber was unable to muster for Alex had entered the womb and developed in little Sarah. She knelt and gave Sarah a long hug.

"You're my special girl," Alex muffled into her auburn curls, "I've missed you."

"I've missed you too. Hey, want to see Ryan's new teddy bear? Grandma gave it to him. I got a new Barbie." A little hand wrapped around hers and they were off to the family room.   "Daddy, look who's here!" Sarah called. Don stood at the hearth, poking a waning fire. A twinge of sadness hit Alex on seeing him. It had always been Dad who tended the fire on cold wintry holidays. He wouldn't let anyone else touch his " Shillelagh" as he called the fire iron. Don came forward and gave Alex a quick handshake and hello. This was only the sixth time Alex had seen Don face-to-face since he married Amber and moved her to Colorado. He still carried the sheepish, apologetic demeanor of a child who has done something bad. Granted, Alex hadn't been overly supportive of her younger sister marrying a man she'd met on the internet. They had only been acquainted for five months when the wedding was announced. Their choice to move so far away had crushed Constance. But for Alex, Amber's departure had meant little. Her younger sister had always made it clear that she was not interested in Alex's life. While their lack of closeness had bothered Alex at one time, she eventually blamed it on the gap of ten years between them.

The kitchen phone rang and Alex heard her mother's voice cheerfully answer. Alex sat on the floor next to Ryan and rubbed up and down his back. So vulnerable, his little body warm and soft, his back not much bigger than her hand. She had to admit, Amber and Don made beautiful babies.

"What a lovely teddy bear," Alex remarked. Ryan looked up at her with eyes like blue marbles and squeezed his toy close to his chest.

"I can't believe it!" Mom's voice wailed from the kitchen followed by the slam of the phone receiver. "He's not coming," her voice trailed off into a sob. "He's got better things to do with his *day off*."

"Michael." Alex gave Don a knowing sigh and headed for the kitchen to console her mother. Amber was already at attention, one arm around her mother's shoulders and the other offering a dishtowel to dry her eyes.

"Now," Amber cajoled, "he'll probably show up late just like he did two years ago. Remember? He said he wouldn't come, and then showed up just in time for leftovers." Her mother shrugged her away.

"He said he doesn't *recognize* Thanksgiving. How can you not recognize Thanksgiving for God's sake?

He could at least come over and eat with us. It's that girl. She's made him go to her family's for all the holidays and we won't see him anymore." Sarah had quietly entered the room and stared at her Grandma with eyes longing to help but not knowing how. Constance caught her concern, and regained composure.

"It's all right," she reasoned. "I have the rest of my family here."

Sarah smiled in satisfaction. "We're family," she assured. The women responded with soft laughter.

"Yes, we are," Alex said.

"Speaking of that," Amber interrupted, "I understand you invited someone special to join us today." She gave Alex that "I know more than you think I do" look that caused Alex to shoot a warning glance toward her mother.

"I didn't say anything," her mother responded innocently. "I just mentioned you were seeing a man from your office who might come for dinner." The end of her sentence was aimed into the oven as she opened the door to baste the turkey. Warmth drifted past, carrying the scent of roasted turkey and sage-spiced dressing. "Why is it every year my turkey takes so long to get done?"

"Because you open the oven door every ten minutes and let all the heat out," Amber said. "Now, what about this guy from work?"

"Oh, he's a friend I've been seeing for about a month—he's divorced and I thought he would be alone on Thanksgiving."

"So why isn't he here?"

Alex felt testiness rise but bit her tongue. *Why should you care?* she thought. Amber wasn't asking out of concern, but rather to rub in the fact that Alex was spending another holiday without a man.

"He's in Oregon visiting his parents."

"Ohhhh, another long-distance family. See, Mom, I may not be the only one to move out of state."

"What are you talking about?" Alex countered. "I'm not marrying him! Besides, he lives here."

Amber grinned slyly. "We'll see. So, Mom, where do you want these serving bowls?"

The next two hours were spent in the ritual of setting the table, passing dishes, coaxing the children to eat something besides dressing and cranberry sauce, and cleaning up the remains. The dinner conversation danced around the periphery of life, occasionally threatening to touch on something meaningful but quickly retreating to complacency.

"How's work?"

"Has Sarah made any new friends at school this year?"

"Mom, your dinner is wonderful as always."

"You really should pay someone to clean the gutters to avoid problems this winter. Perhaps the lawn service fellows will do it."

After the work was done in the kitchen, the family settled on sofas and recliners in the family room. Don had rejuvenated the fire. Crackling flames drew hypnotic stares from the adults. Constance sat on the couch cradling the sleeping Ryan in her arms while Sarah sprawled on the floor busily practicing coloring inside the lines. Alex quietly absorbed the scene— studying each face. How much softer her mother's eyes became with a child in her arms. How unfair of Amber to rob her of treasured grandchildren by moving so far from home.

What of her own treasure? How different would her days be, Alex pondered, if she had a husband and children to share her home and her life? Would having them make her happier? More fulfilled? She watched Amber and Don. When shopping and when attending church or social events, Alex studied families and noticed the interactions between them. She concluded they seemed no happier, no more content than she. No. It seemed to her that people were caught in their own little box whatever shape it may be, all striving to break free in abandonment, all admiring the apparent benefits of another's reality. Everyone was too caught up in the urgency of each day to notice the riches that shaped their existence with character and significance. A few rare souls were able to savor their own surroundings. She knew Dad would be enjoying this day with hearty appreciation. The holidays seemed almost drab without him.

"Too bad Dad can't be here to see how the babies have grown," Alex offered.

That was a grave mistake. The very energy of the room lifted its hackles and bared its teeth. The softness of her mother's face disappeared abruptly. She slowly propped Ryan against the sofa and began to leave the room.

"I'll go and get the coffee started."

An uneasy silence remained until she left the room.

"Why do you have to ruin everything?" Amber accused in a fierce whisper. "Mom was feeling just fine until you had to bring up the fact that Dad isn't here."

"Mom isn't just fine!" Alex responded. "She hasn't been fine in two years. Ignoring reality won't make things better. We owe it to Dad to remember."

"Great. I'm sure he appreciates it. Except Mom's the one left to deal with it."

"But she's NOT dealing with it. Do you know his clothes are still in the closet? She still uses his mug for her tea every morning. It's not healthy."

"That's just her way of remembering. It's not your concern how she handles her grief." The tense conversation woke Ryan and he began to whine. Amber perched him on one hip and bounced softly to quiet him. It worked.

"Two years is too long. She should have moved past that by now. It's not normal to not be able to talk about it, not even show any emotion." Alex could not hide the shakiness in her voice nor the moisture that welled in her eyes.

"I'll go help Constance with the dessert." Don quietly left the room.

"Maybe you're the one who still needs to deal with Dad's death," Amber sniped.

Alex knew Amber didn't intentionally mean to be patronizing and hurtful, she was just so skilled at it she didn't know anything else.

Alex stood to face her sister. Tears began to slip down Alex's cheeks despite her struggle to restrain them. "Oh, what would you know? You're off in Colorado raising your family and completely out of touch. I'm here for the day-to-day and I know what I'm talking about."

"So, now I'm a bad person for living in Colorado."

"That's not what I meant."

Sarah, troubled by the disagreement, stood clutching Amber's leg, a look of fear on her face. In the heat of conflict, she chose her mother. A child will always choose Mother. Alex gave Sarah a soft smile to let her know everything was okay. Sarah returned the smile, but her eyes remained full of concern.

"Maybe you should think about leaving the wonderful Midwest. It might do you some good," Amber said.

"Sure, run away. That's this family's answer for everything. Just ask Michael." Alex shot back. She plopped back on the sofa and looked away, then got up again. "I'm going for a walk. I need to take a walk."

"Talk about running away," Amber giggled with nervous tension and stroked Sarah's long hair. "Don't be gone too long. It's cold out and Mom will worry."

Alex entered the kitchen where Don and her Mother were cutting slices of pie. "I'm going for some fresh air, I'll be right back," she said. Alex cupped her mother's face in her hands to ensure eye contact before slipping on her coat.

Alex stuffed her hands in the pockets of her long coat. The night air, refreshing at first, chilled up her sleeves and down the back of her collar. She wished she had a hat to snuggle down around her ears and quiet the thoughts that bounced in her head.

"That's what Grandma meant," she said aloud. "Put on a hat to muffle the thoughts." She found herself walking the path to Parkdale Elementary, as she had thousands of times in childhood. Neighbors' homes lined each side of the narrow street, their windows intermittently revealing families in various stages of celebration. Every home seemed to say, "Welcome back." Always the same, but never again the same. Alex wondered how many original families still populated these streets. The Parkers, the McCartheys, the Palmetos, so important in her life at one time, now only memories though they still existed just moments away. Alex pondered how people come and go and, sometimes, come back again.

Reaching her elementary alma mater, Alex settled on a playground swing and kicked at the dirt.

"Sorry, Dad," she whispered in the darkness, and immediately decided she would not bring him up to her mother again. She would tuck the treasured memories inside the shroud of pain that, though waning, still lingered, and keep them deep within her own soul. Alex rocked on the swing for a long while until the growing chill compelled her to walk the few blocks back home.

Chapter Ten

The house smelled wonderful! Rich, smoky pine emanated from the Christmas tree and vanilla candles spiced the air. Einstein sprawled on the top of the couch, his eyes following Alex as she bustled through the house, talking to herself.

"Let's see, thirty-five minutes on the pork chops. Ice, I need to make ice. And there should be two forks on the table, one for salad and one for the main course. Oh, and don't forget to get the CD going before dinner." She hurried about the kitchen, making everything perfect.

Though Alex was a decent cook, it had been a while since she planned such a special menu for company. Corey had come for dinner once a week until visiting his parents in Oregon during Thanksgiving. Between her work projects and his, they had spent little time together since. Now it was only one week until Christmas, and Alex wanted to surprise him with a romantic evening and special fare. Cherry sauce to accompany the pork, spiced with a touch of nutmeg and cinnamon, warmed on the stove alongside mashed new potatoes laced with leek and garlic. Everything was in its place and sufficiently elegant to grace the pages of a women's holiday magazine. Pine garland, dotted with blood-red berries and delicate white rice lights, hung around the door frame to the dining room. Soft candlelight threw splashes of yellow against the walls in every room. Alex had even purchased new holiday china for the table settings and unpacked crystal goblets from their storage boxes to sparkle in preparation for the Pinot Grigio they would hold.

"This is actually fun," Alex told Einstein, stopping to stroke his chin. Even fighting with the heavy Christmas tree, which had littered the house with pine needles, had renewed her energy. She had not put up a tree in years. Preparing for the holiday was much more enjoyable knowing the festivities and pleasant atmosphere would be shared with a good friend—a friend she hoped would remain a special part of her life forever. It didn't hurt that the friend was an eligible bachelor and so very available, she mused to herself as she built a fire in the fireplace, a peaceful smile on her face.

The doorbell was Alex's cue to rush into the dining room and turn on the music. Nat King Cole's sultry voice carried "The Christmas Song" into the foyer as she opened the door. A large peach-and-cream-swirled poinsettia, topped with a pair of brown eyes, stood on the other side.

"Oooh, how lovely!"

"With many complements of the season," Corey said as he handed the plant to Alex and stepped inside. She set it on the floor and slipped the coat from his shoulders, planting a gentle kiss on his lips. They felt cold.

"You're freezing! Come in, come in. Come and see what I've done." Alex grabbed his hand and led him into the cozy sitting room. Corey stood at the entrance, silent, surveying the beautiful scene. He turned to glance at the set table, colors from the Christmas tree lights dancing in the glass and porcelain. Alex laughed in childlike excitement.

"What do you think? Does it put you in the holiday mood?" Corey looked at her with soft eyes. His lips tightened.

"I didn't expect all this, just a simple get-together like usual. It's just…"

"It's not that much. Just some holiday cheer thrown in." Still full of energy, Alex fluffed a pillow on the sofa and invited Corey to sit. "Visit with Einstein for a few minutes. I'll get us some wine." Corey plopped on the couch and laid his head back, letting out a long sigh. Einstein immediately curled on his favorite lap for a snuggle.

"Rough day?" Alex asked.

"No, not really. I just have a lot on my mind lately. You know, Jason has been acting up at school for the past several months, but since the Oregon visit it's gotten worse. He's mouthing off to his teacher and picking fights with some of the boys. Last week I met with his teacher and his principal. That's never a fun experience."

"Did you come up with any solutions?" Alex handed Corey his wine and sat beside him.

"Well, I can't threaten him with Santa Claus; he claims he doesn't believe in that sort of 'baby stuff' any more. And it's tough to ground an eight-year-old when he's only around every other weekend. So, we had a man-to-man talk."

"And what did you discover?"

"That he's afraid."

"Really, of what? Has he been watching scary movies? Some of those images are much too disturbing for children and can really bother them..."

"Afraid his mother or I will leave and never come back. Afraid that one or both of us will die."

"Is that what he told you?"

"In so many words, yes. But, I assured him that his mother and I are not planning to run away unless he comes along, and that neither of us is in ill health or ripened to the age of maturity to worry about that sort of thing." Alex chuckled as Corey swallowed his wine. She enjoyed his dry humor and the slight sense of sarcasm that emerged when he was agitated. He did seem out of sorts this evening, not his usual playful self.

"Do you suppose our seeing each other has upset Jason or Derek?" Alex asked. Corey shifted into the corner of the couch and Einstein dropped to the floor to find more interesting endeavors.

"Oh, I doubt it. I haven't really talked about it enough for the boys to be upset."

"Perhaps during the holiday break we can do something together. It will give them a chance to meet me and dispel any questions they might have. They would love the arcade in the mall, or maybe a 'non-scary' movie?"

"Hmmm." Corey looked into the fire and swallowed more wine. Silence rested between them as both fell to their own unexpressed thoughts, watching the flames stretch and bounce between the logs. Alex glanced toward the foyer and noticed Einstein intimately rubbing his face in the poinsettia plant.

"Einstein!" She jumped from the couch, dropping a half glass of Pinot Grigio in the process, and ran to pick up Einstein. "No, that's not for you."

"What's wrong?" Corey followed behind.

"The poinsettia plant. I've heard they can be poisonous to cats if they eat the leaves."

"Oh, God. I'm sorry," Corey stammered, "I didn't think. I'll take it with me when I leave."

"No, really, I love it. I have plans for it at the office." Alex plopped a kiss on Einstein's cheek and sent him on his way, setting the offending plant on the mantle. "He won't jump here; he's too lazy for anything higher than the couch." Alex turned to see Corey grinning wryly at her chest. She looked down to find her silk blouse spotted with white wine, and a few clumps of white fluff from Einstein's belly. Alex fell into embarrassed laughter just in time for the oven timer to announce the pork chops were ready. She scurried to the kitchen to turn off the oven.

"I'll run upstairs and change; you take this towel and wipe up the carpet for me," she said when she returned. Alex changed into a festive red turtleneck sweater, not as sexy but certainly comfortable. She freshened her lipstick and checked her hair in the mirror before heading back downstairs to get dinner on the table. She found Corey already seated.

"Alex," his voice was soft and fresh, but carried a tone of weightiness. "Alex, I need to talk with you."

"Sure." A question mark punctuated her response. "Is everything alright?"

"Everything is fine. Come, sit with me."

"Can we eat our salad while we talk?"

"Sure." Alex took two plates of greens, dressed and ready, from the refrigerator and set one at each place. She stared at Corey, waiting for him to start. It was obvious that he was struggling to find the words.

"You know that my sons are very important to me," he started, "and that I would do just about anything to make their lives better."

"Of course. You're a wonderful dad."

Corey winced at her reply and continued. "Well, Karen and I had a long discussion during our vacation in Oregon."

Alex bristled. "Karen was with you in Oregon? I didn't know…"

"Yes. She wanted to see my folks again and the

boys were so excited that we were taking a trip to-gether, I couldn't refuse." Alex felt as if the air in the room had thickened and tightened around her middle like a corset. "She left her boyfriend six months ago," Corey continued. "He was verbally abusive to her and the boys."

"Well," Alex said, feigning relief, "It's good that she left him then." A bit of silence, then Corey reached over and placed his hand over hers.

"Alex, we're talking about starting over, trying again. Mostly for the boys' sake, but…" Alex pulled her hand away and rested it in her lap, turning to look at the glowing fireplace rather than meet Corey's eyes. So this was it. Karen's presence had lingered around Corey like a virus waiting to take hold since that first dinner at Luigi's.

"Do you love her?" she asked. "Or, should I say, did you ever stop loving her? Or maybe it's just infatuation with something you know you can't have?" Her hurt and anger seeped through her voice despite efforts to restrain them.

"I know this is difficult, but Karen and I have a history together and the living results of that history are being wrongly affected by our behavior. It's our responsibility to correct it."

"*Our* behavior!" Alex snapped. "If I remember correctly, you weren't the one screwing around."

"Yes, our behavior. I gave up too easily because I felt defeated."

"How noble of you," Alex retorted. "Too bad you

didn't think of that before you involved me!" She took a long, slow breath. *Careful, don't sound like a spoiled brat competing against two little boys for love and affection.* Perhaps she had over-estimated this relationship all along, presuming that Corey's feelings were the same as hers. No, he had let himself enter into the joy of another relationship while still haunted with unjustified guilt over his failed marriage.

"Don't you realize how hard this is for me?" Corey said, his voice becoming tight. "I have grown very fond of you, I have begun to love you," and with that he quickly looked away to catch himself from showing the full intensity of his emotion. "For that reason I didn't want to drag this out any longer. It would just bring more pain to both of us."

Alex looked directly into Corey's eyes, confused as they were, and nodded in agreement. "You're right. You have to do what's best for your family." She stood from the table and Corey followed. "I hope you don't mind if I seem a bit removed for a while. I need time… time to process everything."

"Yes, I understand." Corey walked to the door and retrieved his coat. They stood together for a moment in awkward stillness, neither of them knowing how to respond to the other, so they did what seemed appropriate when parting from a friendly stranger— they shook hands. Alex watched Corey's back as he headed down the driveway, then softly closed the door. She felt shocked sadness, then agitation, then pure anger at being emotionally used and misled. She stomped to the mantle, grabbed the poinsettia and hurled it out the front door. The porcelain cache pot smashed on the porch steps with a loud crash as the plant bounced down the walkway leading to her front door.

"Aaaaugh!" she yelled and slammed the door, glad that Corey was already gone and did not see her display. What a waste. A waste of time, of caring, of energy, and of hope. Alex was furious with Corey for giving in to Karen's whims, but respected him intensely for putting his sons above himself. Unfortunately, she had been caught in the crossfire and lay wounded and bleeding, dealing with the results as she best she could. The fact that it was friendly fire made the wound all the more unbearable. Alex prided herself on the fact that she had not shed a tear in front of Corey. Now, she needed a diversion to keep from breaking down. She tried to make light of the evening, to minimize what had just occurred by talking to herself.

"All that work!" she muttered at the lovely table, "and no one to appreciate it." Then an idea popped into her head. It was still early—perhaps Sue and Paul had not eaten yet. She phoned Sue and it was agreed that they would be over within a half-hour to share dinner. Alex quickly removed the evidence of her broken heart from the front porch and set another place at the table.

Once in the foyer, Sue craned her neck to peek into the adjacent rooms. "Where's Corey?" she asked.

"He couldn't make it. It's just us three tonight."

Sue gave Alex a 'there's more to this than you're telling me' look that only women who know each other well fully understand. "That's too bad. Well, perhaps we'll see him another time. Oh, look, Hon! Isn't her tree beautiful?" Paul followed Sue into the family room and sat on the sofa while Sue cooed over the ornaments.

"We haven't had a real tree in ages, since the last one left pine needles in the carpet until June. The guy at the tree farm tried to tell me, 'Lady, you'll regret the blue spruce for the needles,' but it was so perfectly shaped I couldn't resist." Alex sighed in relief to hear her friend's senseless chatter. It soothed her raw soul and helped her forget her loss, at least for now.

"This is a unique ornament. Alex, isn't this your necklace?" Sue lifted from the tree a gold chain that had been draped over a branch, adorned with a golden heart etched with leaves and a tiny citrine stone dangling from its base. Alex had forgotten. She placed the locket on the tree where she could see it and could anticipate a holiday shared with Corey.

"I thought it looked best on the tree." Alex busily put steaming bowls of food on the table to avoid discussing the topic further. "Dinner's ready." Paul rose from the couch, exclaiming how wonderful it all looked. Sue lingered by the tree studying the locket, picking at its clasp until it fell open in her hand, spilling its contents onto the floor—a pinch of sand from the Lake Michigan shoreline.

Chapter Eleven

The next several weeks plodded along with Alex putting in long hours—in part because of her heavy workload, but more to avoid thinking about the miserable holidays. The news of the press release had died down, yet a sense of unknowing and insecurity hung in the air despite all of Seaton's assurances. Alex didn't mind. Riley's plans were developing nicely and, regardless of what happened at Barringer, she would be out of it. Just another month or so until Riley would move into his new office and she could resign. Spring would bring a fresh start. With Riley's instruction, she had contacted her largest accounts and secretly brought them into her confidence. All but one had agreed to move with them. This bolstered both her sense of security and the feeling of approval that she cherished.

Avoiding Corey at the office proved awkward at first, but by the end of February she had become quite skilled at timing coffee and lunch when he would not be in the break room. The two interacted as pleasant acquaintances when forced to. She had lived through the worst incident within a week after returning to the office, when caught at the coffee pot with Corey and Parker.

"So, I hear you're getting back together with your wife." Parker had exclaimed. Corey nodded.

"Yep. We thought we would try to make a go of it."

"Good for you, old man! She's pretty hot. I wouldn't give that up either if I were you." Alex had smiled coyly at them both and slipped from the room. Fortunately, only Sue knew of her involvement and her bruised emotions.

Avoiding Corey was one thing, avoiding Parker was another. His ego stroked by Riley's offer of employment, Parker stopped in Alex's office several times a week to discuss the new venture. She would shut her door and tell him to lower his voice; they couldn't risk news spreading just yet, not until Riley had worked out the client purchase with Barringer's officers. Alex had taken only Sue into her confidence. Because of their friendship, she knew that Sue would never do anything to risk ruining this opportunity for her. Even so, she had only discussed it outside of the office.

"Why not just iron out the purchase now?" Parker protested.

"Because if they refuse to sell the accounts, he will have to breach his non-compete and hope for the best. In the meantime, Barringer will contact our clients and try to manipulate them to stay. He has to wait until everything is in place to move."

"I don't know if I like this uncertainty, though we should be able to get some new accounts with my help," he said. Alex had to admit, Parker was a good talker and had no problem convincing wary firms to give Barringer a shot at their business. He would do the same for Riley's company.

"Any new venture has some risk to it. You have to decide if the risk is worth the eventual reward of seniority with a successful company run by ethical and intelligent management," Alex answered. But Parker did have a good point. It would be reassuring to know when Riley planned to discuss the account purchase with Barringer. She would give it another week before approaching Riley. There was no point in pushing the issue.

Before she had the chance, Parker was in her office again. Reserved, less excited, he shut the door and sat across from Alex.

"I accepted another offer," he started. "Clark's firm called me last week. They have a sales director position open and it's too good to pass up. I mean, it's more money than what Riley offered, and the company's been proven."

"Does Riley know?"

"Not yet. I'll let him know this afternoon. It's a great opportunity, a great firm. I just can't pass it up." Clearly, Parker needed to justify his decision, to feel reassured about turning Riley down. For the first time, Alex realized that Parker needed her input and thought of her as a sounding board in this uncertain situation. Barringer wasn't fond of keeping consultants on the payroll once notice had been given. This would probably be the last time she would see him, at least in a non-competitive way.

"Do you want my opinion?" she asked. Parker nodded.

"I think you need to do whatever is best for you and your career. If that means joining Clark, so be it. Riley will be very disappointed and it will make the start-up even more difficult, but he's a good person and he'll understand." Parker settled back in his chair and nodded.

"Riley will have to understand. Sales director positions don't come along every day and Clark has a good reputation. They needed a decision this morning."

"You're doing the right thing," Alex assured him. Parker stood to leave and Alex reached out to shake his hand.

"Congratulations," she said. "Just be sure to stay away from my accounts."

Parker chuckled. "Sure, sure."

It had been ages since Alex had enjoyed a run. Crisp, cool breezes stroked through her hair and tugged her windbreaker as she jogged over the paved bike path. The parkway was deserted, except for an occasional car gliding past. Mud puddled over the path where the snow had recently receded and broken branches from winter winds littered the patchy grass along its borders. Alex breathed rhythmically, taking in the organic scent of thawing earth. Though a bit stiff from months of inactivity, she felt good—able to enter into the mesmerizing zone where thought disappeared and she knew only the pulse of her breath and the forward thrust of her steps. *If my body would let me, I could do this forever.* She succumbed to the trance, allowing only enough thought to find her way back to her front door and into the kitchen, where she sat until the spell was broken.

The phone jarred her to reality.

"Sorry to bother you on the weekend," Riley apologized, "but I wanted to give you a timeframe. I have a meeting with Seaton Friday morning to tell him my plans. If it turns sour, I'll be leaving that afternoon and, most likely, you will be too."

"That should be fine. I told you that all but one account agreed to come along, didn't I?"

"You did. Most of them realize it's in their best interest. With Parker gone, there are only a few consultants left who could absorb the business and give them the attention they need." Alex wondered if Corey would be assigned to contact the clients and entice them to stay with Barringer. The thought ran contrary to how she envisioned Corey in relation to her: a friend who could have been a life partner. She hoped Seaton would assign someone else the task of being the appointed enemy of her new venture.

"So, Friday it is," Alex confirmed. "I'll be ready for anything. Do you think I should take part in the meeting with Seaton? At least you would have some moral support."

"I appreciate that, but, no. Let me deal with Seaton. We should be fine. He's sold accounts to departing consultants in the past. There's no reason he shouldn't do it now." Alex hung up the phone feeling excited and nervous. What would be the worst scenario? Seaton could refuse to sell the accounts to Riley and pursue a lawsuit against him, and her, for breach of contract. If the clients backed out and stayed with Barringer, they would have some time to acquire new clients. Riley had been secretly working with a few prospects that, if acquired, would provide sufficient income for a time. Alex had analyzed her finances before confirming her decision with Riley. She could get by for five months with no income, living off her savings. After that, she would have to cash in her 401(k). Once that was exhausted, she would be looking for a new job. Knowing that she had left Barringer to chase a fleeting opportunity could cause other firms in the industry to forgo hiring her. Such firms were few and far between as it was. Alex slumped into the kitchen chair and tossed her thoughts back and forth. *Let's just pray that it all works out. God, you have to let this work. Nothing else has lately.*

Monday morning dragged into existence. Dreams barraged Alex's sleep and would not relent throughout the night and into the early morning.

She awoke at nine a.m., more than two hours late, exhausted and out of focus. Deciding what to wear was an effort.

"What is my problem today?" she inquired of Einstein. "Must have been the run and staying up too late. I feel like I have a hangover and didn't get to enjoy the cause." Three cups of coffee later, she arrived at the office ready to go. She passed by Riley's office on the way to her own and found the light on, but him absent. He was not in the copy area or the break room. A few more final questions had developed from the restless thoughts that had kept her from sleep. She wanted to catch Riley while they were still fresh in her mind.

Alex found it difficult to focus on her work and settled on reviewing a contract, slowly, to ease into the day. Several hours later, she looked up to see Sue standing at her doorway.

"Hey. I got in late and missed lunch today. How was your weekend?" Alex asked.

"Oh, it was fine. Quiet." Sue entered the office, softly shutting the door before taking a seat.

"Alex," she started, "Riley's been in Seaton's office all morning and the last half hour has been pretty heated. Riley just stormed out."

"Oh, no!" Alex became pale at the news. "He told me yesterday he was meeting Seaton this Friday to iron out everything. Why would he tell him today?"

"Actually, Seaton called the meeting. I heard him

call Riley into his office."

"But, how would he know? No one knew about this except us, and Parker." Sue raised an eyebrow.

"Well, I can promise you that I never said a word to anyone. Paul doesn't even know."

"I'm not accusing you," Alex assured. "If anything, Parker may have slipped when giving his resignation."

"Are you sure 'slipped' is the right word?"

"Could you hear what was said?"

"Just toward the end when they were yelling at each other. Riley said Seaton was being unreasonable and wasn't following the precedent that he had set. Seaton said he could do anything he damn well pleased and had the non-compete to back him up. There were some other expletives that I don't care to repeat." Sue looked apologetic.

"Did you see where Riley was going?"

"No. He just walked out of the office ten minutes ago." Alex looked through her window to study the parking lot below.

"I don't see his car. Do you?" Sue came to the window to help look.

"No, I don't either. Don't worry, I'm sure he'll cool down and come back. He has to get his things. Just lay low. Perhaps he'll come back after hours when everyone has gone and you can talk with him then, or give him a call at home tonight." Alex was shaken, but listened to her friend.

"Okay. You're right, he has to come back to get

his things. Maybe Seaton will change his mind. It could still work out." The two women looked at each other for a moment, knowing the chance of things working out as planned was about as slim as snow in July.

"I'll call you if anything else happens, and you do the same," Sue assured as she opened the door to leave. "Hon, are you going to be okay?"

"I think so. There was always a chance this could happen. I just don't know yet."

Alex left a message on Riley's phone to call her, leaving no hint that she knew what had occurred. She pretended to work, reading and rereading the same contract paragraph over and over, unable to concentrate. It was almost five o'clock before Riley called her extension.

"I need to talk with you. Come on down to my office when you get a chance." Alex did so, and found Riley emptying his credenza into a box.

"What happened?"

"I never had a chance to negotiate anything," Riley responded. "He knew about our plans to leave and took the position that our entire intent has been to screw the company and steal the accounts."

"Did you tell him you are willing to buy the accounts?"

"Of course, and I reminded him that he sold entire books of business to Dave Clineman and Marty Miller five years ago when they were approaching retirement. He said that was different; Barringer had initiated the offers because the company was going to downsize anyway."

"And they're not now?" Alex asked.

"Don't count on it. Listen, Alex, he's going to impose the non-compete full-force, and use the corporate attorneys to fight us. All I'm coming away with is a handful of accounts that were mine when I joined the firm and my personal prospects, if they decide to give me their business."

"We talked about this possibly happening," Alex answered, "and that we should still be able to move forward."

"He's already talked to our clients, including Tri-Plex, and advised that he would hold us in breach of contract. He's convinced most of them that we would be unable to support a lawsuit and stay in business and has secured written confirmation from them to keep Barringer on through the course of appointment." Alex stood, dumbfounded, at what had taken place behind the scenes without a clue to her or to Riley.

"What now? What does this all mean?"

"It means you can't go."

"What?"

"You can't go," Riley repeated. "The condition of my leaving with the accounts I brought with me is to leave alone. The non-compete says I can't 'entice any employee' to leave for a period of two years." This was a turn of events neither of them had anticipated.

"I thought you had worked the non-compete out

with your attorney and would be able to fight it!" Alex almost shouted at Riley. He just looked at her apologetically and continued packing. Seaton had taken him by surprise. Now he had to ensure his own survival.

"After all this time, preparing, talking to clients, now you tell me I can't go," she said. Riley nodded. His packing finished, he came around the desk to shake her hand farewell. He put a hand on her shoulder and looked sternly in her face.

"I'm sorry to have to leave you behind, but not to leave this place," He said. "You'll be fine. The only advice I can give is 'Beware the Ides of March.' Alex felt defeated and frustrated as she returned to her office. She had been prepared to deal with a fight, but not to be trapped where she was. She became aware of her pen, stilled clutched in her hand through the entire conversation, and threw it forcefully against the wall.

"Damn!" she shouted and buried her face in her hands. She could hold back no longer; tears ran down her face, try as she might to hold them back. Sue appeared at the doorway. It was after hours by now and she had stayed to see her friend through. Her eyes were large with concern as she watched Alex struggle to compose herself.

"They won't let me go," Alex calmly shared. "Not for two years." Sue clucked and shook her head.

"Sue, what does 'Beware the Ides of March' mean? I've heard it before but can't place it."

"It's from Shakespeare. Caesar was stabbed in the

back by his best friend, Brutus, on some date in March. What was it, the thirteenth, the fifteenth? I can't remember. Why?"

"Riley said it just now. I'm not sure what he meant." One thing Alex did know was that the reason she was being forced to stay was not because of Barringer's understanding and appreciation of her role there as much as it was a ploy to hurt Riley as he strived to establish himself. They wanted her accounts to stay; she was secondary to the decision.

Seaton called an impromptu meeting the next morning to explain Riley's departure. Barringer employees packed the boardroom, standing against the walls when all possible room for chairs disappeared. Alex stood at the back of the room, dreading what Seaton might say about Riley, and if she would be implicated in yesterday's events. Pleasant laughter and chatter filled the room until Seaton interrupted.

"You may have noticed by now that Riley Connor has left the firm," he began. Alex drew a long breath and waited for the worst. After a brief description of the number of years Riley had served the company as a senior consultant and his successful recovery from heart surgery last year, Seaton got to the crux of the meeting.

"Riley elected to partially retire, working on his original accounts part-time. Barringer was unable to accommodate his request of a partial retirement, so he has taken a full retirement from the firm and will serve his personal accounts independently." Alex was relieved and surprised at the believable story Seaton was able to weave. No mention was made of her plans to accompany Riley in his new venture.

"Of course, his remaining accounts will be reassigned immediately. I will be meeting with the consultants to review their workload and find an appropriate home for each client." The focus of the meeting over, people began to stir in their chairs.

John Tierney spoke up. "Why don't you reassign all the accounts?"

"What do you mean?" Seaton asked.

"Well, there's no one left on that team anyway to handle the work. Or, who is left probably won't be for long."

Alex flushed. Did she actually hear him right? Would Tierney make such a blatant, derogatory comment about her in front of the entire company? She realized he had. The room fell silent. Several faces looked briefly at her and then away, as if feeling her embarrassment. Seaton stammered for a moment. For once, he was speechless.

"That's it," he announced. "See you all at the next sales meeting." Alex slipped down the hall toward her office alongside several other employees.

"Boy, that was a slam," a young client rep commented to Alex as they walked down the hall.

"Wasn't it?" she answered. "I don't quite know what to make of it." The rep shook his head in disbelief. Back in her office, embarrassment and anger surged within as she thought about Tierney's comments. "No one left, anyway," he had said. So, she

145

was no one, useless. She'd had enough of being discounted and ridiculed by that man. Emboldened by indignation, she marched toward his office to tell him what she thought. She found him in the hallway on his way to the break room, a cluster of employees nearby waiting to refresh their coffee. Alex stood before him, almost too angry to speak, her voice shaking.

"I don't know what your issue is, but that comment was totally uncalled for!" John stared at her in disbelief while the break room crowd hushed. "There's plenty of this team left, and you're looking at it. How would you know what my intentions are?"

John was surprised by her outburst. "I just meant that… you can't stand here and deny that you wouldn't follow Riley wherever he should happen to go," John countered.

Alex shook with fury. "You," she stammered, "are an egotistical bastard! Go to hell!" She turned abruptly, stormed to her office, and grabbed her purse and keys. Sue rushed in behind her.

"Where are you going?"

"I just have to leave for a while. I have to go." She pushed past Sue and hurried to her car. Too agitated to go home, she drove around aimlessly and ended up in downtown Royal Oak. Normally bustling, this chilly midweek afternoon allowed for plenty of parking. Alex stopped for a bagel and soup and then roamed through the shops, her temper slowly easing into dull distraction by the beautiful artwork and antiques she found. The town reminded her slightly of

Saugatuck / Douglas, but with a railroad track running through it instead of a Lake Michigan tributary. Her heart leapt to see a boutique window decked with a collection of the most intriguing hats she had ever seen. The bell chimed in welcome as she stepped inside, breathless, not knowing where to begin.

"Do you mind if I try some of these on?" she questioned the shopkeeper.

"Not at all, I'll be toward the back if you need anything." Proudly displayed on wooden and wire stands, tucked among handbags, teacups and silverplate, each hat told a story of its own heyday. A plain black felt fedora from a time of rationing and war tilted its brim as if to show off its sexy yet tough demeanor. Next to the fedora a crimson saucer hat snapped at conventionality—a striking statement from the frivolous 1950s, neighbored by a soft feather-brimmed cream picture hat from the same era. This was the one she selected and carefully arranged on her tousled hair. She glanced into a nearby mirror. Charming, but off the mark without the appropriate slick French twist and red lips to accompany the look. Smiling, Alex fondled and studied each prospect. She had to take at least one home and, considering the morning's events, perhaps it would be a few. She stepped away from the front room to investigate the rest of the shop. More hats, and clothing too, filled the hallway and adjoining rooms. A large-brimmed sun hat constructed of variegated crocheted granny squares hung over the door, reminding Alex of the mid-1970s and the excitement of moving up to junior high school. The shop was lined with small rooms full of character and history. It was pure heaven.

"Finding everything all right?" said a voice coming from the back.

"Oh, yes. This is wonderful! You have so many nice things."

"Thank you. Enjoy looking—that's how we meet some of our best customers."

"Do you have many customers who, I mean, do any of them actually *wear* these hats?"

The shopkeeper looked around the doorframe from the back room to make eye contact.

"Well, I'm not sure what they do with them once they leave, but we do a pretty good turnover. Most of them come from estate sales or folks bring them in to sell."

"You certainly have a new customer in me," Alex said warmly. She entered the last room and shuffled through a rack of vintage dresses and wispy underthings in delicate peach and pearl, so very feminine. A flash caught the corner of her eye. She turned to see a baby pink pill-box with delicate veiling sprinkled with pink crystals. It sparkled in the dim light as if trying to get her attention. Alex let out a slow, long breath as she walked toward it. It reminded her of Grandma. The sight of it brought a memory into clarity—once again she felt the excitement, heard the sounds and smelled the scents of the shopping trip just before Easter when she was only five years old.

Her grandmother had bought such a hat, and a white straw number with navy blue sash and two silk daisies dangling from the ends for Alex to wear to church on Easter Sunday. Such a day they had, wearing their new hats proudly out of the shop, stopping for an ice cream sundae at Saunders on the way home. She had felt like a princess. Grandma always made her feel special and loved. A refined woman, and only in her early fifties when Alex was a young child, she had always worn a dress and hat, and smelled of White Shoulders and pressed cotton.

Alex turned the hat over and over in her hand, fingering the price tag, the numbers smearing together as her eyes moistened. *I wonder if this could actually be Grandma's hat,* Alex thought. She could almost feel her grandmother standing nearby, watching as Alex gazed at the little pink hat. Perhaps Grandma's spirit had even drawn her here, called her attention to it, as a reminder that she was watching out for her still.

"I'm so confused, Grandma," Alex whispered.

Within the silence of the tiny room, her mind could hear the tender voice respond. "I know, dear, but don't you worry. Everything is going to turn out all right." Alex smiled and, clutching the pink pillbox hat as though it was a long-lost treasure, headed toward the counter.

"Will you be wearing this one?" the shopkeeper asked.

"Oh. I don't know. My grandmother had one just

like it, and I do collect hats. 1 will probably display it." The shopkeeper nodded in approval as he took Alex's money and gingerly wrapped the hat in tissue paper. As Alex stepped out into the evening, the setting sun cast a golden pink glow down the sidewalk, illuminating the sides of each building and tree to an almost unbearable brightness. Alex stepped briskly toward her car to avoid the March air.

"Everything will be all right," she repeated. "Boy, am I ready."

Chapter Twelve

At fifty degrees and with the sun shining, it was an uncommonly warm Friday in March. The pleasant day made it difficult for anyone at the Barringer Group to concentrate on work. The handful of employees still there at three o'clock found excuses to get up for a drink or to mill over to the next office to chat about weekend plans. Alex strolled down to Sue's office for a brief interruption and found her busily stuffing presentation binders. Only Sue could have so much energy on a Friday afternoon.

"Hey, aren't you about ready for the weekend?"

"No." Sue was standing behind her desk, frantically sorting her presentation into six binders yawning open on her desk. "I have a meeting first thing Monday morning, and I really don't want to have to come in tomorrow to finish it."

"I'll leave you alone then."

"No, really, stay and visit for a bit. I can talk and

151

sort at the same time."

"Why don't you have the clerk do that?"

"She said she didn't feel well so I let her go home." Sue leaned forward and lowered her voice as if sharing an international secret, "that time of the month."

"Oh, in that case..." Alex smirked. If she had taken the day off every time her period made her feel like she was ready to explode in pain, she would have used every sick day ever granted. "So, what are your plans for the weekend?"

"Nothing interesting. Saturday I'm getting ready for our church rummage sale. There are boxes Paul and I never unpacked when we bought the house in Plymouth—I'm sure there are plenty of things we won't miss. On Sunday we're having Paul's folks over for dinner. How about you?"

"I have absolutely nothing planned."

"Hmmm." Sue snapped the binders shut and piled them on the corner of her desk before flopping into her chair. "Want to help me go through boxes? I'll make you strawberry shortcake." Alex laughed at her friend's bribe.

"Sure, I'll come for a while, and you don't have to feed me." Their conversation was cut short when Kate Rossman entered Sue's office with two un-known men, all three dressed in business suits.

"Excuse us, ladies," Kate purred, "We'll only be a minute." Then, addressing the two men, "this is one of our smaller offices but, being next to the executive suite, it could be expanded to make a larger work center." The men nodded and smiled at Alex and Sue, one of them scribbled a few notes on a legal pad and they were off down the hall. Sue looked at Alex, her eyes wide.

"What was that all about?" Sue asked. She then shot from her seat and peeked around the doorframe to see where the trio went next. Alex followed. Kate and the two men were studying the cubicles in the center of the office, talking, nodding, and scribbling.

"Maybe we're moving. Is our lease expiring?" Alex wondered.

"Not for five more years. Well, whatever it is, we'll find out before too long. I'm either getting promoted to a 'larger work center' or moved out the door."

Saturday repeated the sunshine and warmth that brings Michiganders out in droves after being trapped indoors for months. Still too cool for much outdoor activity, the roads were full of people just wanting to get out of the house. Alex headed to Sue's home at eleven o'clock to help sort through potential rummage sale paraphernalia. A small box of her own contributions sat on the back seat: a set of stemware, a small white enameled mantle clock that no longer suited her décor, and a box of costume jewelry that she found attractive but always forgot to wear. At the last moment, Alex added another item to the box: an empty heart locket necklace with citrine stone. She wouldn't be wearing it again, and it should fetch a nice price for Sue's church.

"This is perfect!" Sue took the box from Alex as she entered the front door. Charlie whimpered and paced until Alex stooped to rub his massive head between her hands.

"Yes, you're a good doggie, aren't you?" she crooned through puckered lips. Sue continued to talk as she walked into the dining room, Alex and Charlie following her voice.

"The historical home and garden tour selected to include our home this spring. I have so much to do between now and the end of May I don't know where to start!" Sue babbled. Alex and Charlie stood watching until Sue looked up, triggering a sniff from Charlie.

"I brought all these up from the basement," she continued. "If you will just empty them onto the table, or where ever you can find room, I'll sort through it and decide what to keep and what to donate."

"Great. Where do I start?" There were at least ten boxes on the table.

"Anywhere is fine. That one, I have no idea what's in it," Sue pointed to a box at the corner of the table. While Sue corralled Charlie out of the room, Alex ripped packing tape from the box and began emptying its contents onto the dining table. That done, she moved to the next.

Sue had returned and began moving boxes to the floor. "We're going to need more room on this table."

"Here," Alex said, taking a box from Sue's arms. "Let me do that. You start looking through what I've unpacked." Sue sat at the table in front of the first box-ful while Alex transferred one box at a time from the table to the middle of the adjacent living room floor.

"Ooomph. This one weighs a ton! It must be full of books." As Alex dropped the heavy parcel on the floor, she heard a faint whine from the dining table. Sue sat, pressing a tiny pink cardigan scattered with embroidered flower buds and trimmed with buttons no bigger than a ladybug into her face, desperately trying to stifle her sobs. Alex stood, puzzled, watching her friend hide her face behind the tiny sweater, then walked over and put her arm around Sue's shoulders.

"What? What is it?" Alex cajoled. Sue needed a few moments to regain composure before easing the sweater from her face. Not noticing earlier, Alex took a closer look at the items she had unpacked from the 'unknown' box. A delicate christening gown and bonnet wrapped in cellophane, a stuffed wooly lamb and several children's books were scattered about the table.

"Oh, look," Sue sniffed, "I got mascara on it." Alex pulled up a chair and waited for her to explain. Sue looked at Alex's concerned face and managed to laugh. "It's okay. I'm okay. It's just…" she looked as if she might cry again. Alex waited patiently, quietly, for Sue to continue.

"I bought these things the first year Paul and I were married and set them aside. We didn't try for the first few years because he was finishing med school. When he finished his internship and went into practice, we tried to get pregnant. After two years, we found out our chances of having a baby of our own were slim."

"I'm sorry." Alex interrupted.

"That's only half of it," Sue continued, "Two years ago, we went through many tests and decided to go ahead with artificial insemination—and it worked! I was pregnant for four months. I had just started to show... that's when I had the miscarriage.

"Why didn't you tell me?" Alex questioned.

"I don't know. Denial, I guess. Somehow, I felt like I killed my baby. I had forced her into existence, and my body couldn't carry her."

"You know that's not true," Alex protested. "You had every right to try to conceive. It's not your fault things didn't work out." The two sat in silence for a while, absorbed in their own thoughts.

"Do you ever miss it?" Sue asked.

"What? Not having children?"

"Not having children, not being married."

Alex snorted. "Sure! Actually, I thought about adopting a baby when I reached my thirties and knew there were no marriage prospects on the horizon. But then I realized it would be difficult to raise a child alone with my work schedule and little family support, so I dropped it. I think we're wired to be mothers and to nurture a family. But, you know what? There are a lot of things out there that need nurturing. I nurture my clients, an occasional plant, and you've seen Einstein!"

Sue chuckled.

"It's a matter of looking at your life and working with what you have," Alex continued. "No one promised us as little girls that we'd all grow up to be wives and mommies some day. We just believed it was a given."

Sue nodded in agreement and wiped her eyes. "Miracles can happen."

"Yes. So, you'd better put these aside for safe-keeping." Alex stacked the children's books and carried them and the rest of the baby items into the kitchen. She knew there were no good answers to give her friend who was still hanging onto the hope of motherhood. Thank God she had moved past that; past the grief and consternation, until finally giving in to the fact that she would never be someone's mother. Oh, there was still some time left, but it was scant little. So she had desensitized herself to the urges within. She no longer felt the waves of longing pulse through her heart that sent her spiraling into depression every time she saw a baby. She accepted, almost relished, her independence now. Of course, a small part of her soul had not given up on finding a meaningful relationship with a man. Though close to death as well, a faint breath of yearning hung on. She almost wished it would die and let her live peacefully in her solitude.

Alex and her mother clinked glasses of brightly-colored alcoholic drinks decorated with paper umbrellas over a celebratory dinner. The Chinese restaurant was crowded and swelled with voices and laughter.

"I'm proud of you, Mom," Alex said. "Here's to your first step toward the future." Constance giggled a small youthful laugh that Alex remembered fondly.

"Your dad's clothes were taking up an awful lot of space in the closet. I just decided that someone could be getting use out of those things. You know, one day it dawned on me that I could look at those clothes and smile over the good memories instead of cry, and that it was silly to hang onto them a day longer."

"Well, I'm glad. Dad would be happy for you."

"You know, he would! I could almost hear him joking about it, saying 'so, you planning on wearing these anytime soon?' He was always so sarcastic." Constance was becoming loose-tongued, though she'd only managed to sip half of her drink. "Oh, I almost forgot!" she reached for her purse, pulled out a wad of tissue paper and handed it across the table to Alex.

"What's this?"

Her mother shrugged and took another sip of her drink. Alex pulled away the tissue to find a gold pocket watch and chain with 'Carl' engraved on the ornate cover. She gasped and tried to stifle a laugh while tears simultaneously sprang to her eyes. "Mom! I can't accept this." Constance wrapped her hand around her daughter's, enclosing both their fingers around the timepiece.

"Please, take it. I want you to have it."

"Well, all right. Thank you, I will treasure it always," Alex said as she carefully wrapped the watch and slipped it into her purse. "By the way, I have something for you, too. It's in the car. I wanted to give it to you later, but I can't wait." Alex babbled like a little girl excited over a handmade Mother's Day gift. "Wait here, I'll be right back."

"What is it?" Constance urged.

"You'll find out in a minute!" Alex hollered over the noisy restaurant crowd as she moved toward the door. She returned with a round box covered with white toile in black-print roses and held together by a red cord. Alex handed the box to her mother, then plopped back into her seat.

"All this running around and your food is getting cold," Constance teased as she lifted the lid and separated folds of tissue paper. "Oh my, what's this?" A cherry-red designer hat with sheer net veiling dropping off the brim emerged. "It's lovely! But, do you really expect me to wear this?"

"No. Not really. That's not the point. It's what it represents."

"And what is that?"

"Life. Just enjoying life." Constance perched the hat at an alluring angle on top of her head and laughed.

"Like this?" she asked.

"Yes, just like that." Alex's eyes sparkled at her mother's joy.

159

The Ides of March had arrived. Riley had known this was coming; Alex suspected but failed to subscribe reality to her intuition. Even with Seaton mentioning a pending restructuring months ago, she had put it aside in hopes that the situation would play out differently. Alex had denied the truth since it first appeared wearing a red dress and blowing its own horn. Seaton called a meeting to announce The Barringer Group had been purchased by Rossman, Kidwell and Sparks. There would be a "restructuring of personnel," as he put it.

"Does that mean layoffs?" one bold employee called out.

"Yes, there will be some terminations." A pall fell over the group. Alex wasn't worried. She had more seniority than everyone in the room save John Tierney and had a nice group of accounts. They would need her expertise and her clients. Hopefully, the law firm would allow the acquired employees to stay in the area and would not move them to one of their out-of-state locations.

Within a day the terminations began. The Human Resources director from the new parent company set up in the conference room. Employees knew they were on the list if they received a phone call from extension 201. The voice at the other end politely asked them to step down to the conference room and, within twenty minutes, the employee would be packing their desk. The only consolation was the severance benefit which included one week's pay for each year of service.

Alex sat at her desk, caught up in the tension, listening to the mayhem unfold. A phone rang in the cubicle just outside her door and a young female clerk cried out in a shaking voice. This was too much. Alex had to get out of her office. She took the elevator to the first floor and stepped outside for a brisk walk around the building. As she walked, a faint, nondescript song whistled in the air. It became louder, and Alex scanned the sidewalk and parking lot but could find no one. The song broke, and then continued, and she realized it came from above. Alex craned her neck, looking up at the glass-encased building. A window washer, bundled from head to toe against the March wind, sat on a scaffold just three floors from the roof. His equally bundled partner, a girl appearing no older than her mid-teens, stood leaning over the edge of the roof, slowly easing the rope from the strong metal arch that craned over the building's frame. The girl whistled each time the rope was let out, and then stopped when the scaffold came to rest. Was she his daughter, perhaps? While the window washer had the more precarious job, the young lady watching his descent was the more nervous of the two.

The scene made Alex think how it seemed preferable to experience a trial yourself than to watch a loved one experience it. When in the thick of adversity, she mused, the act of living through it and finding a solution is more tolerable than watching from a distance. Everything can change so quickly and without warning. There is no real security, no real trust to be found in anything but your own abilities.

She decided there, shadowed by the place where she lived fifty hours a week, that if she were to stay on, there would be changes made. She would take her vacation, even if only to weed the flowerbed in the backyard, and she would create a life outside of work.

"Seaton's looking for you," the receptionist said as Alex returned to the office. "He's in the conference room." The conference room! Alex caught her breath and tried to hide her surprise. She headed for the conference room to find Seaton and the Human Resources director seated at the table, her employment file before them. Seaton stood to welcome her.

"Alex, come in. This is Frank from Rossman, Kidwell and Sparks." Frank stood, his eyes large behind dark-rimmed glasses, and shook her hand. "Now, this isn't what you might be thinking," Seaton assured as he pulled out a chair for Alex. "Frank here has a position for you under the new management, and he wants to talk to you about it." Well, that sounded hopeful. Alex smiled at Frank as he began.

"We have an account representative position available that would allow you to work with your existing clients and new clients as they are acquired." Alex dropped her smile. "You would be paid a scheduled salary rather than commission, with opportunity for bonus if you are directly responsible for bringing a new account to the firm." Frank's voice faded away. Alex digested his words.

"You mean," she said, "I would not be directly consulting with clients?"

Frank looked away and tossed his head, struggling for the best way to stretch the truth. "Not directly, no. You would work alongside a consultant who would be chiefly responsible for the accounts." Alex couldn't believe what she was hearing. They were offering her nothing, a demotion—a move that would set her back more than ten years. Years of experience in a position in which she was good—damned good.

"What about my clients?"

"You'll still be able to work with your clients," Seaton interjected, "just not in the same capacity."

Alex slumped back in her chair and stared at the two men incredulously. "I can't accept this!" she responded, straining to keep her voice calm. "You're asking me to give up a senior consultant position and the ability to control my income, for a fixed income as an account rep?"

Frank responded first. "There are only a few consultant positions available and they are all filled. We are offering you a good opportunity with a good firm…"

"It's not an opportunity, it's a concession," Alex interrupted. "Can I ask who has filled the consultant positions? Would Kate Rossman happen to be one of them?" Frank shifted in his seat and refused to answer. He slid a letter across the table in front of Alex.

"This is our offer. We need your signature on the last page if you accept, and we'll need your decision by the end of next week."

"And if I don't agree with the offer?"

"We have to fill the position as proposed to you." Frank answered. Seaton sat silently. He no longer had any input or control. Alex took the letter, assured them that she would respond by the following Friday, and returned to her office.

Her faced flushed with the rejection. This slight was more hurtful than any thing she had ever experienced before. After investing the past ten years of her life in doing her utmost for Barringer Consulting Group, they were tossing her aside and discounting everything she had accomplished. Embarrassment and anger kept her glued to her chair, unable even to share with Sue what had just happened. She wondered who the chosen few would be. Which fortunate scavengers would benefit from her years of hard work and relationship building? Corey? John? Kate?

All at once Alex began to doubt her abilities, her value, and her very worth as a woman. What was left, if not her career? What now? She buried her face in her hands and quietly sobbed, tears dropping on the papers strewn over her desk, over Frank's letter, the words smearing together in a squiggle of black on white.

The following Friday took a lifetime to arrive. Alex deliberated and procrastinated throughout the entire week. *Lots of people are looking for good jobs,* she thought. *I should be thankful*. When at last it came, Alex dressed in her best power suit, black with a white silk blouse and black patent pumps, and headed for Barringer, soon to be RKS Consulting, with resolve. She drove in silence; no radio today to add distraction.

"Where's Seaton?" she questioned on finding his office empty.

"You didn't hear?" Sue offered. "He was 'retired' yesterday."

Alex sniffed at her friend's choice of words. "Another one forced out, eh?"

"You look nice. Have an appointment today?"

"Just with destiny."

"Oh. In that case, he's in Parker's old office."

Frank stood in welcome as Alex entered the office.

"I've made my decision. Here you go." She tossed the letter on the desk. Frank picked it up and immediately shuffled to the last page.

"But, you haven't signed it." He held the letter out to her.

"Right. I don't intend to." Frank sighed and dropped his hands on the desk.

"Are you sure you've thought this through? Do you know what you're doing?"

"Absolutely. I should ask you the same thing. You're letting a proven employee walk out the door. It doesn't have to be like this."

"Yes, I'm afraid it does."

"Then, you have my answer." Alex started to leave.

"Oh, and I'll be pursuing my severance package."

"There's no severance if you've turned down a valid offer of employment."

"No, I've been terminated. You terminated me by eliminating my position and I'm entitled to a severance just like every other terminated employee." And with that, she left the office and walked through the double glass doors that had bid her good morning and sent her home day after day. There was no need to return to her office; she had removed the few personal effects the day before. Her knees trembled just a little as she stepped through the doors for the last time, calling on her remaining vestige of inner strength and self-respect as she walked away. Alex knew a large part of her soul would remain there, but only until she was ready to call it home again.

Chapter Thirteen

Hot August sun broke through the morning haze and lifted the scent of blueberries on the air. The only sound came from a pair of katydids calling to each other across the tall maples lining the farm. Row upon row of tall bushes heavy with leaves and berries engulfed Alex as she searched for the best fruit, her tennis whites glowing on the sandy soil. A large-brimmed straw hat sheltered her face and neck from the late-morning sun, and a white bucket tied around her waist hung heavy on one hip, filled to the top with blueberries. Clusters of berries clung to the branches in various stages of ripeness, from small mauve pebbles to plump, fleshy morsels almost black, all dusted in translucent white. Alex popped a large specimen in her mouth, crushing it between her teeth to release its sweet juice.

"Mmmmm," she breathed, closing her eyes as if sight would distract from the experience.

"Heavenly." Blueberries back home didn't taste like this. She picked more than she would be able to eat in the two remaining days she planned to stay near Lake Michigan. The couple who owned the bed and breakfast would appreciate the results of her labor. The experience of it was so enjoyable, she could have picked blueberries all day. She found it mesmerizing, like a meditation that takes you to a place from which you don't want to return. Alex slowly walked toward the white clapboard barn to weigh and pay for the contents of her bucket. How refreshing it was to have nowhere to be, nothing she had to do. The lazy summer afternoon yawned before her like an empty country road begging a walk. Alex had spent the early part of the week browsing the shops of Saugatuck / Douglas, watching sailboats skim across the gentle evening waters of Lake Michigan, thrilling from a dune buggy ride along the sandy hills and enjoying early-morning runs along the shoreline. Aside from the dinner cruise scheduled for the next evening, she had experienced much of the tourist fare and was beginning to feel like a regular.

The hot sun and Maria Von Paradies' "Sicilienne" soothing from the CD player made her eyes heavy as she drove back to the romantic B&B only steps from the Lake Michigan shore. A nap sounded great. She would freshen up later, go to dinner, and then walk to the shore to watch the glowing pink sun settle into the lake as the lavender sky turned to turquoise then black.

The room was cool and welcoming when Alex returned from dinner. Elegant navy and periwinkle threads swirled on the bedspread across a four-poster bed, loaded with matching pillows. A Jacuzzi tub waited behind two white columns in one corner of the room. Perched on the back corner of the Jacuzzi, a cluster of pale violet wisteria held by a cream-colored ceramic vase bowed their heavy blossoms as if to admire their reflection in the water. On the adjacent wall, a gas log fireplace waited, its mahogany mantle ornamented with antique books and a pair of crystal candelabras. Alex really didn't need all this luxury for her one-week reprieve, but when making her reservation, she had found herself asking for room 10. She needed to see this room again, alone, to create in her mind a different memory of it and to erase the vision of an October night spent here resting in Corey's arms, awakening to the enthralling dream of a meaningful life together.

Now was a time for new beginnings. She would return home to a new consulting job at a competing firm. After a few months clearing her head of Barringer cobwebs and interviewing for a new position, Alex had come to the charm and rest of Lake Michigan to create fresh energy for her new endeavor, and to say her final goodbye to the one lingering tie that incessantly interrupted her thoughts with regret. She checked her face in the mirror before heading out for the evening. Her cheeks glowed from the summer sun and outdoor breezes, a splash of tiny freckles playfully scattered across her nose. She replaced her lipstick with a translucent pink. An older, more serene woman stared back at her. No, only her eyes looked older. Not in the way that aging lends lines or puffiness, but from the well of her eyes emanated a sense of wisdom and understanding, a look that said, *I have been there and survived.* She sighed and gave her reflection a slight smile. "Ali, you need to lighten up."

She placed the room key, her money, and I.D. in the pocket of her cotton sundress—the less she had to carry around the better—and headed down the staircase, through the flower garden, and toward the lively main streets of Saugatuck.

"I'll try the Traverse City cherry," Alex requested, pointing at the tub of vanilla ice cream swirled with red cherry jam among rows of options tucked behind glass. "In a sugar cone, please." Why not live it up? The streets were full of locals and visitors delighting in this warm Friday evening. Couples and families strolled along the sidewalks, spilled from shop doors, and lingered in the mouth-watering aroma of grilled steaks, salmon and tomato sauce that enticed them through restaurant doors. Laughter and applause lifted on the lake breeze, carried from the shoreline park where a musician sang to accompany his acoustic guitar. Alex strolled slowly through this menagerie, licking ice cream as it softened in the warmth and trickled down the sides of the cone. A few puffs of clouds had developed over the lake and

Alex hoped they would not hinder the view of the sunset, still an hour away.

White benches dotted the park's edge along the harbor. She planned to sit and admire the sights until time to head for the shoreline near her bed and breakfast, but felt restless and decided instead to wander the sandy shoreline, to watch the gulls chase and listen to the rhythmic "swoosh" of the waves as they rolled in and ebbed away. Selecting a complimentary folding chair from the inn's porch, Alex headed toward the beach.

Though a small public site, the beach access was tucked within a lakefront neighborhood and felt secluded. The public beach was flanked with private properties. Wooden steps twisted up the steep banks, leading to majestic homes hidden within tall maples and oaks, their large-windowed rooms surveying the lake's expanse. Alex wished she could live in one of those homes, and never have to leave this place. She removed her sandals and kicked through the warm sand, looking for the best spot. A handful of admirers were already scattered along the shoreline, standing or seated toward the lake to enjoy the sunset. Alex chose a spot at the water's edge and settled in her chair, chilly Lake Michigan waves licking her toes.

She sensed a person standing behind her without hearing any approach. It was a vague feeling of a presence that she shrugged off, refusing to turn her head to see if it could be substantiated. She waited a moment and heard the faint squeak of a folding chair opening and the rustle of a paper bag.

"Mind if I share a seat next to you?"

The familiar voice overcame her heart. She jumped and turned to look at his face.

"I'm sorry. I didn't mean to startle you." Corey apologized.

"No, I just didn't expect anyone. Why are you here? I mean, how did you know I was here?" Alex stammered.

"Sue. I asked her and she told me you were on vacation, here. She didn't want to at first, but, well, you know Sue."

"Oh. Sure, sit down." Corey wrestled his chair open and sat next to Alex. "When did you arrive?" Alex asked, pleasant but detached.

"About an hour ago."

"Oh."

"Looks like the clouds may cheat us out of a sunset tonight," Corey said, squinting at the fuchsia sun ball, now dropped considerably toward the shimmering water, pale gray clouds inching toward its path. Alex glanced toward the sun and made no comment. The two sat in silence until the glowing orb, half-cloaked in clouds, inched toward the water and finally dipped its edge in like a shy child entering a swimming pool.

Corey turned toward her, attempting to make eye contact, "Listen, Alex. I came here to look for you, to let you know I've made a serious mistake." Alex shot up from her chair and started walking down the shoreline. Her haste caused cold water to splash up her calves and she retreated to the sand. Corey followed.

"No! No! NO!" Alex turned and yelled at Corey, her arms pushing him away. He stood, determined yet silent. "You come here," Alex's voice broke, "you come here like nothing has happened and expect me to just let you in again!" Her arms swung wide as she exemplified her point. "What do you think I am?"

"Someone I'm in love with," Corey answered.

"Hmph." Alex snarled and walked away. "You've already got one of those." Corey followed close behind.

"No, I don't. I realized after trying to live with Karen again that I don't love her. I'll never be able to love her again." Alex kept up a brisk pace, but Corey had caught up and walked beside her as he continued. "We decided months ago to just leave it. The boys will be okay. They were worse off when we were together, always miserable and bickering." Alex stopped and looked squarely at Corey. Dusk had tiptoed in and darkened the world around them. Far off in the distance, dark gray cumulus clouds rumbled.

"So now what? Do you just expect that I can turn it back on again?"

"No, but I had hoped you would give it a try."

Alex sighed and stared out at the horizon. "Oh, God, what are you trying to do to me?" She turned to look at Corey. He stood facing her, his bare feet covered in wet sand, his hair disheveled, a hopeful little boy look in his eyes, and suddenly she began to

173

laugh. She laughed at the fact that Corey was here again, in this place, vulnerable and wanting her. She laughed in release: loud, uncontrolled laughter that turned into a sob and then back into laughter. Corey stared awkwardly at first and then he slowly joined in as he realized Alex's anger was dissipating. They stumbled through the cooling sand back toward their folding chairs, moving them away from the now cold water, and fell into them, struggling for composure.

"Okay, sure." Alex said at last. "But you'd better watch your P's and Q's."

"I'll do my best." Corey opened a bag of crackers he had left by his chair and tossed them toward the squealing, chortling gulls that ran along the sand. As the sun sank under Lake Michigan, only a remnant of daylight glowed on the horizon. Soft light emanated from the windows in the trees. Faint flashes illuminated the clouds in the distance, and a warm wind carried the sound of thunder.

Corey lifted his voice over the rollicking waves. "Looks like a storm is rolling in." The gulls, sensing falling night, lifted into the air one by one and flew out over the water. Alex studied Corey's profile, the softness of his eyes and his hair edged along his masculine face, the nape of his neck where her head once rested. Somehow she felt he would be safe——safe to love. He noticed her watching him and slipped his hand toward the arm of her chair to rest it on hers. Alex looked at his hand settled there, and did not pull away. The gesture brought a smile to his face.

"By the way," he said, reaching into the pocket of his jeans, "this belongs to you." He opened her hand and dropped a gold necklace in her palm, a leaf-etched heart with citrine stone dangling from its base. Alex's eyes widened in surprise.

"But I gave this away."

"Sue had it. Something about you setting aside something for her and her wanting to do the same for you…" Corey shrugged. Alex smiled and opened the locket. Empty. She remembered. A well-meaning friend had accidentally dumped its contents on her family room rug. She picked up a pinch of cool sand, released it into the locket and snapped it shut.

As darkness fell, the pair folded their chairs and stood with a small cluster of onlookers to watch the approaching storm. Rolls of dark clouds, illuminated with continuous flashes of lightning, inched across the sky toward the shore. Alex approached the water and stood at its edge, gray waves fighting against gray sky as far as she could see. The back of her neck tingled from the power of it. She stood, defiant of the fear stirred by the violent, noisy clash, until reason told her to back away. A drop of wetness touched her arm, another her forehead.

"It's starting," Corey called out. "We'd better head back." Alex and Corey ran up the winding wooden steps to the street above and dashed under the porch as the storm grew to a crescendo. They quickly returned the folding chairs to the stack and sat on a cushioned porch swing. Sheltered there, in a halo of soft light spilling from the parlor windows be-hind them, they watched as an angry wind howled from the lake and pelted the roof with a loud torrent of rain. Though the night was warm, Corey wrapped an arm around Alex's shoulders. They sat silently, en-grossed in the storm's magnificence. As the thunder began to slip further inland and the rain subsided, Alex rested her head in the curve of Corey's neck, peacefully watching the storm recede.